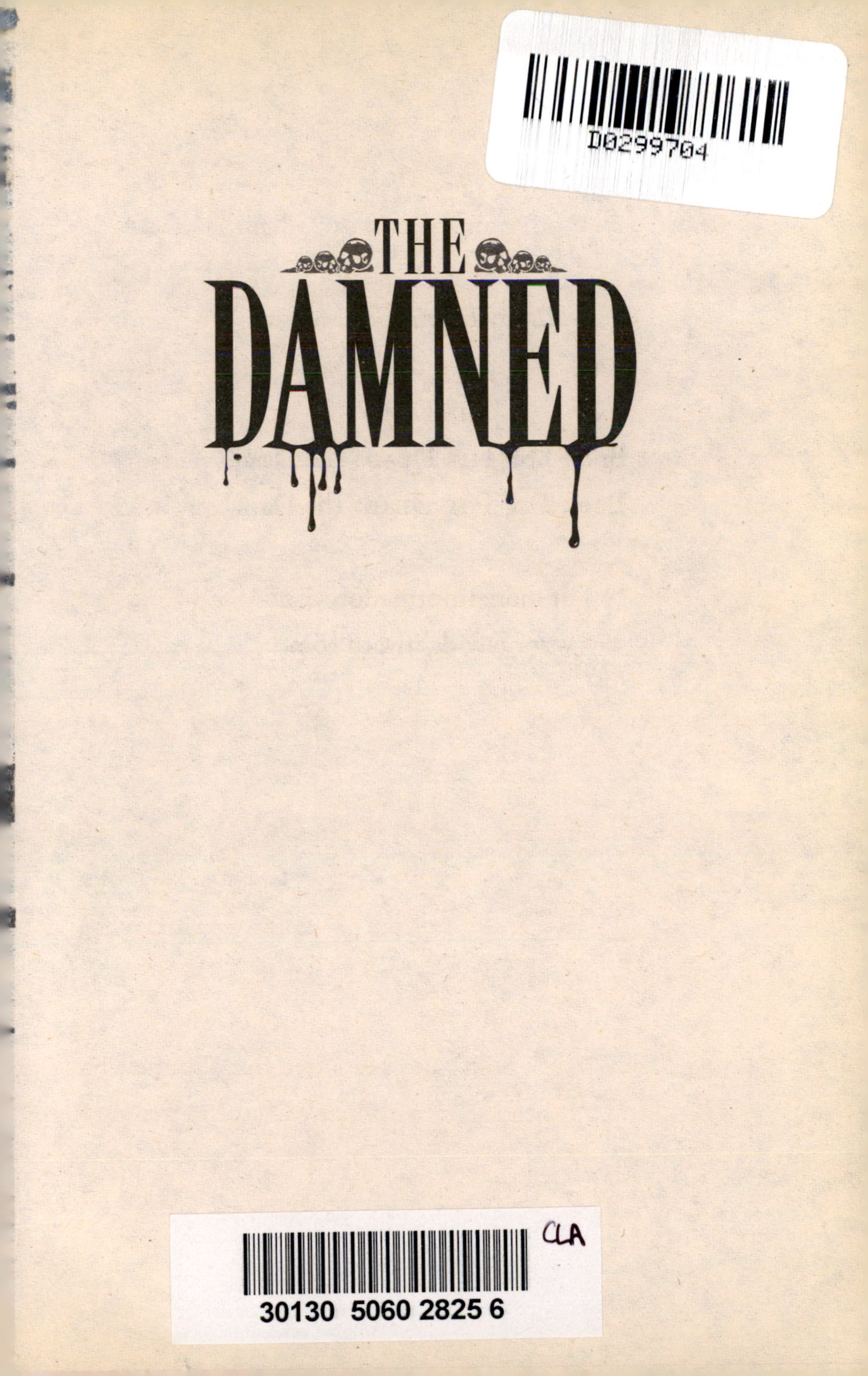
THE
DAMNED
D0299704
30130 5060 2825 6
CLA

Also by David Gatward

THE DEAD

Book 1 of THE DEAD: The Dead

Book 2 of THE DEAD: The Dark

For more information visit:

www.davidgatward.com

DAVID GATWARD

A division of Hachette Children's Books

First published in Great Britain in 2011
by Hodder Children's Books

1

A Catalogue record for this book is available from the British Library

ISBN 978 0 340 99971 4

Typeset in Caslon by Avon DataSet Ltd,
Bidford-on-Avon, Warwickshire

Printed and bound in Great Britain by
CPI Bookmarque Ltd, Croydon, Surrey

The paper and board used in this paperback by Hodder Children's Books are
natural recyclable products made from wood grown in sustainable forests.
The manufacturing processes conform to the environmental regulations
of the country of origin.

Hodder Children's Books
A division of Hachette Children's Books
338 Euston Road, London NW1 3BH
An Hachette UK company
www.hachette.co.uk

Paul 'I paint nightmares on the walls of my skull' Edwards
– I seriously doubt that I would've written this
if I hadn't moved next door to you . . . and stolen all your
DVDs. Your dark thoughts inspire as much as they
terrify me . . .

Nina Bradford – None of this would've been
possible without you, or your love of Brie de Meaux
and a bottle of red . . .

'King's tower and queen's bower,
And weed and reed in the gloom;
And a lost city in Semmerwater,
Deep asleep till Doom.'

Sir William Watson, 1858–1935,
The Ballard of Semmerwater

'And you will face the sea of darkness,
and all therein that may be explored . . .'

Lucio Fulci, *The Beyond* (1981)

PROLOGUE

The scream tore from Abaddon's throat, ripping the night in two. All he saw, all he'd stood for, all he'd come to believe in, smashed into the dirt like a rat under a coach wheel.

The churchyard was thick with the scent of trees hammered by a storm that had raged non-stop for three days, slamming the world into a thunderous sludge. His hands were clawed into soil cut by rivulets of cold, grey water. And deep beneath, the dead slept on. The only warmth he felt was that of the blood running from the two fingers that had been sliced off, moments ago. They lay just away from him in the dirt, pale and dead. From the wound he felt no pain.

Abaddon tried to pull his eyes shut, but they refused and kept on blinking in the damnably cool and refreshing rain, as droplets spilled down his face unhindered. Why wouldn't it stop and give him just a brief moment to cry his own tears? He struggled against the hands that held him, the same hands that had pushed him to his knees and forced him to watch, and wondered if he had any tears left.

'My . . . family . . .'

A dirty breath slumped across Abaddon's face like a drunk steadying himself against a wall; a greasy mix of booze, rotten teeth and fatty meat.

'Forgive me, priest.'

Abaddon managed to raise his eyes. 'You . . . bastards . . .'

The breath got so close Abaddon felt moisture against his cheek, then rough lips and jagged teeth scraped his skin through a thick, matted beard.

'Didn't think your type were allowed to use that sort of language.'

Abaddon's chest tightened as his lungs tried to heave breath after breath after breath, as though doing so could pause time; stop it, run it back just enough.

Just enough; was that too much to ask? He was a man of the cloth, for god's sake! What was the point of believing in anything if something like this was possible? This wasn't supposed to happen to someone like him.

But it had. And the evidence of the violence of the last few impossible, shocking moments was only a few steps away; three bodies slumped like broken mannequins against the church wall, unable to move and take shelter from the rain.

Abaddon struggled to pull away from the murderous touch that held him, but a boot hoofed him hard in the kidneys, and he keeled over into the slurry of dirt and water pooling about him. He coughed and tasted blood.

The water felt inviting and he wanted to drown in it and let the stink of the night slip in and choke him. At least then he'd be with his wife, Anabelle, and two children, James and Mary, instead of here. Alone.

'So you want a closer look? A chance to say a final farewell?'

Abaddon didn't know how to respond. A final farewell to what? Empty caskets of flesh lying broken on a rain-soaked churchyard, their contents spilling silently into the earth? To faces locked in those last moments of horror, eyes staring hard into a world they'd never see again? To everything that had given him a home, purpose, meaning, laughter, pain, hope, understanding, patience, love?

Abaddon shook his head. 'No.'

Even his own voice had changed, as if it had been snatched away from him with his family on the winds of death, to dance to whatever lay beyond this world, never to be seen or smelled or touched again.

'You sure, mate? I mean, I'm not completely heartless. Come on, I'll give you a helping hand.'

Abaddon was lifted to his feet. He had no real idea how his body worked any more. He was separate from it now, as though whatever it did, or whatever was done to it, would never really harm him. Pain had turned into a phantom and he didn't fear it. He was emptiness complete and nothing would ever fill it.

For the first time that night, he was face-to-face with his family's killer. The man had a look in his eyes that thrust a shiver through Abaddon's body like a rusting, blooded spear. Something was beating behind them, a presence that reeked of an evil so overpowering Abaddon nearly gagged.

'Can you walk?'

The sound of the man's voice, so friendly, as though all

this was just one of those things, sickened Abaddon to his core. He tasted bile rising in his throat. Spat.

'Come on, then.'

Abaddon didn't move.

'I'll drag you there if I have to, so help me God!' the voice snapped back.

Abaddon stared at the remains of his family. 'You're beyond God's help,' he hissed, his voice still shifting, breaking on every word like the sea against rocks. 'We all are, now.'

'You know killing you would be easy, don't you? I could take a few more fingers first, get imaginative, perhaps move on to a limb or two. Really drag it out . . .'

Abaddon stared back. He wanted to die. He had nothing left to live for but to bury his own. Pain was nothing.

He was already dead.

The breath moved away and the grip on Abaddon's arms went slack. The man holding them, the leader of the gang he'd found ransacking his church only a half-hour ago, was standing facing the rest of his men. They looked like a row of half-starved dogs, moon-mad and grinning.

'Check 'em,' he growled, and the man's hands squeezed Abaddon hard on his shoulders. 'Make sure they're proper dead. Don't want any runners now. They ain't rabbits to go squealing on us to the rest of the warren, right, lads?'

One of the gang, a fat man whose stride matched that of a strutting turkey, walked over to the three figures slumped against the church wall. He gave each a single kick hard enough to make a living man puke. But when the third kick landed a sound escaped from the body; an impossible croak pushed out of a throat from flesh still hanging on, refusing to quit and let go of the spirit it harboured.

At that sound, the man drew a pistol and placed it against the temple of the body on the ground. He sent a gob of spittle through the air.

Abaddon heard the hammer pull back, click into place, saw time slow to that of a snail's pace. He tried to yell out to prevent what he knew was about to happen.

That breath against his cheek once more.

'Bit of a waste, ain't it, priest?'

'Don't, please, I'm begging you.'

'You want me to let the kid live?'

Abaddon's heart was cracking like rotten wood. He nodded. 'Please . . . she's only seven years old . . .'

'I'll tell you what then,' said the gang leader, his smile snapping each word like a chicken bone, 'I will. As a goodwill gesture, mind. But I'll need a guarantee you won't go chasing after us, doing something stupid, if you know what I mean.'

It wasn't hope Abaddon felt then, at the thought of his daughter surviving, but a lessening of the darkness inside him so faint that even night would not distinguish it. But it was enough and Abaddon clung to it immediately, a drowning man hanging on to the sorriest of branches.

'Anything,' he said, his eyes filled now with nothing but the solemn, pale face of his still-living daughter. 'Anything at all.'

For the first time that night, the clouds cleared and a bright moon flared through the gloom. Abaddon stared once more into the face of his family's killer. Hell stared back and he gasped. Something in those eyes made him feel as if he'd opened a furnace and been blasted by the heat; a thick, suffocating, cloying lust for turning everything that life should be about into everything it should never even witness.

'We'll be taking her with us then!' said the man, and before Abaddon had a chance to protest, broken teeth were revealed behind a crooked smile; tombstones in a dark cave. 'But first,' the man continued, 'we're going to show you something that'll guarantee you'll never chase after us, and never forget what we're capable of. Or who and what we really are!'

The rotten wood of Abaddon's heart turned black.

The leader of the gang nodded at two others who came over and grabbed Abaddon. One rested a cocked pistol against his temple, then the leader walked over to where Abaddon's family lay, and knelt down at the side of his barely living youngest child.

The gang leader nodded to one of the dogs who reached into the bag he was carrying and removed something wrapped in dirty, oily leather, and handed it over. A piece of rock, a thick splinter of black granite about the length of a man's forearm. It looked like it had once been a part of something else, as a series of symbols ran down one side, some of them only half visible, the edge of the shard splitting them in two.

When the splinter was rammed into the ground at the side of Mary's body, and gore from a wound on her arm dripped on to it, Abaddon's blood froze and he released an anguished cry; he didn't want to begin to guess at whatever the hell kind of dark, evil rites were about to be performed on his daughter.

The gang leader looked up and smiled as he stepped back. 'You ain't seen nothing yet, priest.'

At that, something flowed out from the splinter like a thin trail of water; it shimmered for a moment, an odd watery crack in the air. Then the crack split and opened, revealing a swirling darkness behind, and from it emerged something so abominable, so utterly against the laws of all creation . . . Abaddon shuddered and tried to push away from it, his skin crawling.

'In God's name what have you done?'

The thing slipping from the crack was a man. But that was all that could be said of it, for it was a ruined version unlike anything Abaddon could ever imagine. As it dragged itself through the crack, its skin ripping and shredding like it was caught on the glimmering tear that still shone in the air, it first snatched a look at the scene that met it. Then it grinned as it turned to Abaddon's daughter and pulled itself out completely from the tear.

Abaddon watched the tear close, saw something move in the darkness behind it that reminded him of a squid's tentacles rushing to catch its prey, then nothing. Only this thing it had vomited up against Mary.

The gang leader pointed his finger at Abaddon's daughter. 'Fresh flesh,' he said. 'And young. It'll taste good! Think what you'll be able to do! Imagine it!'

The thing grinned, let slip with a laugh of wet gurgles and hacking coughs, then reached out to Mary, and started to push its way into her.

Abaddon struggled. Abaddon screamed. But nothing he could do could stop the horror taking place in that impossible moment of time. And with each push from the creature, as it slipped a little further inside Mary's body, Abaddon watched his daughter shake and buck and flail about until, at long last, the creature was gone.

A moment later, Mary sat up, snapped her eyes open, and someone – some*thing* – else stare out from behind them.

1

PRIVATE DARKNESS

Lazarus Stone was at the wheel of the meanest-looking Land Rover Defender ever built. In the passenger seat was a dead man. Behind him, an angel.

'Abaddon? Abaddon!' He shouted the dead man's name and punched him hard on the arm. It felt like thumping a bag of sand and pain stung his knuckles.

'Wake up, you dead idiot! You bloody well nearly killed us!'

On the seat between Lazarus and Abaddon lay a three-edged spike, about as long as from his elbow to the end of his fingers. The handle was a mass of metal thorns sharp enough to rip his hand apart. Each thorn corresponded to a faint, bloody hole, which sank right through Lazarus's hand. He was half tempted to grab the thing, have those thorns sink into his palm, and ram the spike into

Abaddon. But he'd seen the effect of the spike, used it to awful effect on the Dead. And Abaddon wouldn't stand a chance against it. No one would, living or dead.

Abaddon's head snapped back. 'Mary! Where . . . Oh, God!'

Lazarus was taken aback; Abaddon usually displayed about as much emotion as a lump of granite.

He shook him more gently this time. 'Abaddon?'

Abaddon shook his head and turned round to glare at Lazarus.

Lazarus shivered. Since becoming the Keeper, the one person standing between the Living and the Dead, he'd seen more than his fair share of dead things and hellish creatures, but Abaddon was something more. He made the Dead look tame.

'What happened? Where are we?'

Abaddon's voice was an eerie echo in a dark cave.

'I could ask you the same question,' said Lazarus. 'You've been dreaming.'

Despite having got used to Abaddon's presence, Lazarus was still a little freaked by him. Being dead was one thing, but those eyeless sockets in a skull covered by brown, stretched skin centuries dead sent him cold. They didn't even close when Abaddon rested. And there was the smell of the embalming fluid Abaddon had used to preserve his body. A sort of musky hum of spiced vinegar. It stuck in Lazarus's nose and hung around his throat like the aftertaste of something he shouldn't have eaten. Arielle had led them to him, the scourge of the Dead, a long-dead priest out for revenge on those who murdered his family. He wasn't exactly a lot of fun to be around.

Abaddon's forehead furrowed like damp, crumpled cardboard.

'Dreaming . . .' he said. 'I saw my family. Mary! The village: we must hurry!'

Lazarus focused back on the road ahead. Being just a few days shy of sixteen, hoping the police didn't catch him was one thing, but outside the weather was turning nasty. The rain fell like it wanted to smash everything into a thousand pieces.

'Remind me where the village is,' said Lazarus.

'Hell, Lazarus. You know that.'

'So getting there isn't easy, right?'

Staring through the relentless storm was giving Lazarus a headache.

'Must've been quite a dream.'

'Why?'

'You grabbed the steering wheel is why,' replied Lazarus. 'You were thrashing about like something was ripping your arms off.'

Abaddon turned from Lazarus, clenching both hands, one of which had two fingers missing. Lazarus didn't want to know how he'd come to lose them.

'Memories, dreams, nightmares, they are all the same,' muttered Abaddon, his voice like a whisper leaking from a tomb. 'They are all of them bad.'

Lazarus wanted to ask more but a hand gripped his shoulder. Arielle, his not entirely sane guardian angel, was sitting behind him. Lazarus looked at Arielle's reflection in the rear-view mirror. Her pale skin looked ghostly against the rain-dashed windows of the Defender. Her dark, lank hair fell from her head lifeless and tangled, like seaweed washed up in a rock pool. Then he caught his own reflection in the windscreen. He looked like crap. His black, usually jagged hair matted to his head with sweat and more than a little blood. And his clothes, black as always, looked as if he'd just escaped from a pit filled with barbed wire; they were covered in rips and tears, and his skin was scarred with scratches. Despite being only a few hours old, the wounds had pretty much healed.

Being the Keeper of the Dead had its advantages. He was able to heal more rapidly than any other human being alive. Which was lucky really, seeing as he'd not just been close to death, but shook hands with it more than once. It had something to do with the fact that to sense the Dead, a Keeper first had to taste death. Arielle had given him his *taste*, blasting him in the chest with a pistol before pulling him back from death. Being touched by an angel didn't just heal the soul, but the body as well. What he wasn't so chuffed with was the fact that he could now sense the Dead. If any were near him, he'd know about it, and their presence would be announced by a sudden wave of nausea powerful enough to kick an elephant to the ground in a pool of its own vomit. Thankfully he'd learned to control it, but that didn't make it any easier to endure. Or pleasant.

Arielle asked, 'What's happening?'

Lazarus nodded at Abaddon. 'Just our dead friend here trying to kill us. Won't shut up about his village. You know, the one swallowed by a lake and sent to Hell? Can't see why more people don't just head on down there; must be a blast!'

Abaddon remained still and silent as a statue.

'How long have I been asleep?'

Lazarus didn't have a watch. 'Couple of hours, I guess,' he said. 'Any idea how much further?'

Arielle glanced at Abaddon then took a hit of something alcoholic from a flask she kept inside her coat.

'We are close,' growled Abaddon. 'I can sense it. Everything around us . . . I know this place, these lanes . . . hills.'

Arielle's reflection turned back to Lazarus.

'And you, Lazarus?'

'What, other than hoping I don't get arrested for driving this truck of yours? You sober enough yet to drive? Oh wait . . . you just had another drink, didn't you? Or does alcohol not actually affect angels?'

'Lazarus—'

'And it would be nice to have some idea of what I'm supposed to be doing other than taxi-ing you two from one war zone to another!'

Arielle smiled and Lazarus, rant over, breathed in the stale wine that clung to her every breath. He didn't want to get into how he felt, not now.

'I'm sorry,' said Arielle. 'About your dad. And your friends. There was nothing we could have done, you know that, right?'

Lazarus gripped the steering wheel so hard his knuckles glowed white.

'I never asked to be the Keeper, Arielle,' he said, trying to stay calm. 'But there's no point being it if I can't even save . . .'

His voice collapsed to nothing. From the off he'd only been in this for his dad. And he'd been so close to saving him.

'Everything went wrong, Arielle. Everything! We should've been able to save them but all we did was screw everything up even more!'

He hadn't just lost his dad, but his best mate, Craig, and a new friend to them both, Clair. He choked up, tried not to show it, and failed.

'Do not dwell on what happened,' said Arielle, seeing the flicker of emotion on Lazarus's face. 'We did everything we could. And this is not over yet. Abaddon and I can only do so much. But it is you, the Keeper, who must put an end to this completely.'

'Really . . . ?'

Arielle nodded. 'I know you don't yet know how. I can protect you as best I can, as can Abaddon. We can help you find where you need to be, but only you can finish this.'

Lazarus wasn't listening. Whenever he thought about what it was that he was doing, what had happened, how he was stopping the Dead from returning, he knew he sounded insane. And the awful truth of it was that this was more real than anything he'd ever done in his life.

Arielle's hand squeezed his shoulder. Her grip was so strong it felt like she could have easily just pushed through his flesh and bone.

'Tobias . . . your father, there's still a chance, Lazarus,' said Arielle, her voice soft and caring, but unable to fully cover a hard edge to her words. 'And for Craig and Clair. The Dark took them, but they are not yet dead!

Hold on to that.'

'The Dark took them?' sneered Lazarus, shaking his head. 'How can you make something so awful sound so utterly normal?'

'I'm sorry,' said Arielle. 'I don't mean to blasé.'

'You failed,' said Lazarus.

He would never forget the Dark, that hideous thing that the Dead had turned his father into; a great, stinking mass of everything bad about humanity, and all of it poured into one man to give him the power to smash apart the barrier between the Living and the Dead.

Lazarus knew deep down he would see it again and that terrified him. But if it was the only chance of saving his father and his friends, so be it. If there was something Lazarus had learned about himself these past few days, it was that he wouldn't turn from a fight.

For a while, he stayed quiet; if he even tried to say anything about what was going on in his head, his words would roll around his mouth like a lump of chewy, gristly meat that he'd eventually have to spit out.

He'd uncovered so much about his parents over the past few days, and it was overwhelming. He'd spent his whole life accepting the fact that his mum died when he was a baby and that his dad was a bit weird. Hell, the guy was away most of the time, and when he was home, hardly spoke. But then he'd found out about his dad being a Keeper, and from that moment things had just gotten worse and worse. And nothing could have prepared him for what his long-dead mum had become or what she would do.

Lazarus shivered. His mum . . . She'd used his dad, got him to cross over to the land of the Dead, then trapped him and turned him into the Dark. His dad had lived a lie all his life, thinking the woman had loved him. That thought made the bile rise in Lazarus's stomach.

At last, Arielle's grip relaxed and Lazarus was brought out of the shadow of his thoughts. 'Everything we've learned about your parents has been news to me too, Lazarus,' she said, almost as though she'd read his mind.

Unnerved by Arielle, Lazarus dropped a gear to heave the Defender round a bend in the road. The vehicle drifted a little on the wet road, he eased off the throttle, held it. The road ahead was an ancient scar on the hills, a nasty wound kept open by millennia of traffic.

'Perhaps I should drive.'

'Perhaps you should shut the hell up!'

'Lazarus—'

'I can still smell alcohol on your breath!'

The road straightened out and Lazarus went up a gear and accelerated hard. 'And if it's all the same with you, rescuing my dad, Craig and Clair isn't something I'm about to risk on a drunk driver!'

'I am not drunk!' snapped Arielle, her eyes flaring with fire. 'Now, pull over and let me drive!'

Lazarus enjoyed getting a rise out of her. 'You're supposed to protect the Keeper, right? Then start doing it!'

Arielle said nothing more, leaving Lazarus to his own private darkness.

'You have a plan, right?' he asked. 'I mean, I know that *I'm* supposed to end all this, but I'm guessing, as guardian of the Keeper, you have some clue how?'

Abaddon's skin creaked as he moved to face Lazarus. 'You saw it as well as us, Lazarus,' he growled. 'The Dark has your father and it took the others! This is just the beginning. What it did to them, what it is doing now, it will do to all humanity! All life! Do you understand?'

With Abaddon's voice rising, Lazarus kept himself quiet.

Abaddon hadn't finished. 'There is more to concern you than simply rescuing three people. Being the Keeper is not about helping the few, but the many!'

Lazarus was in no mood for speeches. He was tired, angry and upset.

The Defender rattled over a cattle grid and Lazarus saw some sheep in a field dash away in the rain.

'I'm in this for Dad,' he said, 'and for Craig and Clair; I don't give a rat's arse about the bigger picture! If that means I have to go to this damned village in Hell, fine, but I'm doing it for them and that's it!'

It no longer mattered that his dad had hardly been around. He was the only family he had. He wanted him back.

'Not much you can do about that,' sighed Arielle, sitting back. 'You're a part of it, Lazarus. We know it. And so do the Dead. And, like I said, no one can end it but you.'

Lazarus opened his mouth to say something but

couldn't find anything but swear words. He focused on his driving to clear his thoughts.

Nothing made sense. His life had been easy really. With Dad absent most of the time, he'd been left to his own devices. Money was always there to sort out food. The au pairs hadn't ever been a problem; some of them had even been pretty hot. Craig had become a roommate as much as a friend, spending more nights staying over than either of them really realised. On those occasions his dad had been around, they'd been civil, but little else. If anything, Lazarus knew he'd been treading water, waiting till he could just up sticks and leave, break out on his own and live life his own way.

Now everything was different, messed up, screwed. And here he was, driving to a village in Hell, with an angel in the back and a living corpse in the passenger seat. And all for a dad he hardly knew, a mate who'd got involved in all this by accident, and a young woman who'd nearly killed him.

A gust of wind hooked round the Defender and Lazarus felt the steering wheel pull from his hands, bringing him out of his thoughts, back to the present. The wheels swerved, but he held it as he stared into the swirling rainstorm that was drenching the land around them.

Abaddon's voice slipped through the sound of the rain drumming on the roof. 'Over that hill,' he said, pointing to a distant shadow. 'In the next valley lies our destination.'

Lazarus wasn't exactly relieved, but he was glad the journey was almost over. He was knackered, brain dead and hungry. With the promise of the end in sight, he squeezed the tiredness from his eyes with a hard blink, flexed his hands and willed himself to stay alert. The road ahead was narrowing, so he had to stay online; meeting another vehicle coming the other way would be a narrow miss at best.

The road steepened ahead, and Lazarus dropped a gear to pull the Defender up it with ease, but as he did so, a motorbike burst round a corner ahead, almost lost it as the back wheel swung out, and accelerated hard towards them.

Something smashed through the windscreen, Lazarus's head span with nausea, and gunfire shattered the night.

2
SCREECHING METAL, BLOOD AND BONE

'Arielle!'

The angel leaned over the seat between Lazarus and Abaddon as more gunfire split the air. She grabbed the steering wheel as Lazarus fought to stop himself being overcome by nausea and blacking out.

The Dead were on that bike; living bodies occupied with something that had slipped through the veil between this world and theirs: the swimming sense that he was about to puke told Lazarus that much. It always happened when the Dead were close by. He was dealing with it better and better but this had caught him totally off guard. He did his best to pull himself low, sink deep into his seat and avoid getting his brains blasted out the back of his skull.

'Ram them!' yelled Arielle as Lazarus reached up to take control of the Defender again.

'Are you mental? They're shooting at us!'

'And it's our best way to prevent them scoring a direct hit!' said Arielle. 'Do it! Now!'

Gunfire again, up close and personal. Lazarus turned to see Abaddon pulling his arm back in through the window, flintlock spent.

'I'm not running them over,' Lazarus hissed through gritted teeth, and heaved the Defender to the other side of the road. 'Whoever they are, they're still people!'

'Whoever they are,' said Arielle, 'the Dead have them already!'

'You think I don't sense that?' yelled Lazarus, his mind now clear, but his stomach still churning.

Arielle shouted again. 'Remember what we're dealing with! Like you said, I'm supposed to protect you. So let me! And do as I say!'

The bike adjusted its course. Lazarus saw bullets smash into them, ripping a Morse code of death down the wing in front of him. He swung to the other side of the road again as a gust of wind and rain crashed into the cabin.

'Abaddon, what the hell . . . ?'

Abaddon's door was open and he was leaning out, battered by the rain, and taking aim with a loaded pistol. The ball rammed down the barrel exploded towards the motorbike, caught the one at the front in the shoulder. It burst in a spray of blood, but made no difference; they were still speeding towards them.

Abaddon was back inside.

'Nice shot,' said Arielle.

Abaddon snarled as he pulled out another pistol from inside his jacket. 'Keep her steady, boy!'

'Lazarus! My name is Lazarus, you dead git!'

'Do as I say!'

Again Abaddon was out through the door, and again his round hit home, this time slamming into the bike itself in a crash of sparks.

But Lazarus wasn't looking; ahead he'd spotted a chance to get out of the way before the bike slammed into them: a gate leading from the road through the wall to open moorland.

'You'll never make it,' said Arielle, guessing Lazarus's thoughts.

Lazarus ignored her, gunned it. The Defender seemed to pull itself into the road, like it was ripping it up with its wheels as it heaved forward. The bike was only a second or two away now . . . He could make it. He had to . . .

'Hold on . . .'

With a final glance at the motorbike, registering only that neither rider was wearing a helmet, Lazarus yanked the steering wheel hard. The Defender groaned as the rear slid out. Momentum had it firmly in its grasp now, and the truck just kept on moving forwards.

They crashed through the gate, smashing a section of the wall in the process. In that last moment, Lazarus caught sight of the motorbike, as though in slow motion, as it skidded sideways and slammed down on to the road, and both passengers slid right under the wheels of the Defender. He felt the thump-thump-crunch of their bodies, the motorbike. Then everything went dark.

Lazarus jolted awake so violently he thought his head was about to rip off. A scream pitched itself forward out of him. With his hands still clasped to the steering wheel, he shuddered with the force of it, like his lungs were about to follow through on to his lap.

Rain was spattering against his face. The windscreen had popped out completely on to the grass to his right, smashed and useless. His knuckles were bleeding and the iron taste of blood in his mouth made him cough.

A flashback scorched his brain and the pain of it made him wince. The faint, sweet, sickly smell of death crept up his nose as visions of the motorbike crashing through the wall to a symphony of screeching metal, blood and bone played out in his mind.

He must've blacked out, but for how long? The day was darker now, so long enough for afternoon to turn to the first hints of evening. The world outside was still being battered by the storm, but now the Defender was no defence against it, and Lazarus shivered.

Amazed to have survived at all, he carefully reached down to unclip his seatbelt, conscious that there was a good chance something was broken. But as he pulled himself loose of the strap, all he felt was bruised and battered.

Lazarus turned the key and the engine growled

quietly in front of him, as if it was frustrated that they'd had to stop at all.

With a flick of the light switch the beams from the headlamps cut through the darkness with an intensity that burned away the night.

In every direction lay a bleak world of grass and bracken, broken only by the remains of a wall or the tumbledown carcass of a long-unused barn. It was a landscape staring him in the face, daring him to get lost in it, and sink without trace in one of its many hidden, treacherous bogs. In the distance, the ragged tops of hills that haunted the horizon seemed to be watching him, like they were just waiting for something bad to happen.

A yawn forced Lazarus to close his eyes. When he opened them again he spotted something on the ground to his left; a body, face down, its limbs twisted into positions they could only achieve by being snapped in numerous places. In that same moment he realised that Abaddon was no longer in the passenger seat.

He made to move and go help the dead priest, though if someone's already dead, just how the hell was he supposed to work out if they'd survived being thrown through the windscreen of a vehicle being driven through a wall?

The thought of the crazy situation he was now in brought Craig to mind. Even in this situation, he would have something funny to say. Then thoughts about where Craig was now took everything and crushed it like meringue in a vice. Lazarus choked down the tears. Then heard breathing.

Turning slowly, he spotted the shadow of Arielle in the back of the Defender, lying on the floor like a broken doll. Around her, cans of food lay like fallen soldiers. And her hair glistened with shards of broken glass like ice on bracken.

He pulled himself over into the rear of the vehicle. With an eye out for more broken glass, he reached down for Arielle and lifted her on to the seat. She was so light it was like lifting a child.

He placed a blanket over her to give her a chance against the cold, wet wind blowing through the Defender. All he had to do now was check on Abaddon, see just how bad the damage was from the crash, and then wait for them both to wake up. Beyond that, he hadn't a clue.

He reached for the door handle, but it was jammed. He tried again, but all he got was a sore shoulder and the sound of complaining metal.

He pulled himself over to Abaddon's seat, but as he did so, a figure slipped out of the darkness and rain to stand in the stark bright light of the Defender's headlamps.

When the figure started to walk towards him, Lazarus felt his soul start to burn.

3

'DO NOT BE AFRAID . . .'

Lazarus tried the door again, slamming himself into it, pulling at the handle hard enough to snap it off. His fingers strained, his knuckles popped, but the door still wouldn't shift. Snapping his head round, he shuffled quickly over to the passenger seat, tried Abaddon's door, but that too was jammed. And it didn't even give way when he lay on his back and kicked as hard as he could, like he was trying to kill it, not just open it.

Lazarus turned to the back of the Defender, reached over and shook Arielle. 'Wake up! Bloody well wake up!'

He wasn't sure if it was a voice or a sound or just an overwhelming sense of power, but it latched into him like a fish hook and pulled him back round. Lazarus tried to stare at something else, to gaze down at Abaddon and yell at him to get up and get busy with his weapons and sort out whatever this thing was that was approaching – but it did no good, and he was staring through the broken window, through his only possible means of escape, at something getting closer, something that seemed to be pulling the wind and the rain and the dark into itself, like wherever it walked the world would just let it through, and it was close now, real close, so close Lazarus felt as if what he was seeing now was searing its image on to his very skin.

Warm blood dripped down his arm and Lazarus realised too late he was gripping where the windscreen should've been. Shattered pieces of glass were biting into him, forcing his skin to give way and weep a little. But he didn't care and couldn't feel the pain. Not now. Not with what he was looking at forcing everything else in his head to fade into insignificance.

The figure was not only about three metres tall, but utterly naked except for the long ribbons of blood-soaked hair that whirled and tangled in the wind about its head. And it looked like it had just pushed itself through a whole heap of razor wire, its skin hanging off in bloody, soft shreds. Its face was torn like a bear had mauled it, a deep rip down the middle, red and wrong. But those same shreds and wounds were healing themselves. And as the figure drew closer, its every move delivered with the grace of a dancer, it grew ever healthier with each step, until all that was left of the wounds were scars, and they too were soon fading to nothing but a memory.

The figure paused but a step away from the front of the Defender, its pale skin shimmering with the rain skipping down it, racing to the ground across flesh as smooth and white as porcelain. And utterly hairless. It was lean, muscled without being bulky, built like a triathlete. The features of its face, now completely healed, were neither male nor female, but with a little imagination could've been either. Which, to Lazarus, was at that moment no surprise, when he realised something else about the figure, something shocking. Because who or whatever it was, it had no sexual organs at all.

Whatever he was facing now, it was not of this world. And neither was it one of the Dead. It reminded him of Red, the twisted creature who had turned up with a message for his dad, and started off this whole descent into nightmare and chaos.

But on that occasion he'd smelled death. It was the one thing that confirmed a creature was from the land of the Dead. Or at least from the other side of the veil that sat, invisible, between the Living and the Dead. But there was no smell on this creature, nothing at all. The only faint reek of death was from whatever was left of the two on the motorbike now buried under the Defender's wheels. Whatever this was, and wherever it was from, Lazarus didn't want to know, and was sure as hell that he shouldn't hang around to find out.

He snapped his eyes away from the horrifying thing staring at him and turned to head out through the back of the track, past Arielle, aiming to grab the spike from the middle seat on his way. But as he made his move, he heard the door at his side rip off its hinges. There was no time for shock as the creature grabbed him and pulled him round, yanking him out from the Defender. Lazarus managed to grab the spike and brought it up in a vicious thrust hard enough to gut a wolf. But the figure holding him simply slapped it away, then tore it from Lazarus's hand and threw it into the dark.

Lazarus stared down into the eyes of his assailant. His feet weren't touching the floor. The only thing stopping him falling was the ferocious grip and strength of the creature now holding him. And he knew he was utterly screwed.

'Who are you? What do you want?'

Lazarus struggled against the grip holding him, but it was pointless. He reached round, grabbed the passenger seat belt, anything to give him a chance to pull away. But the figure yanked the whole mechanism from the door pillar.

Cocking its head to one side, and without any hint of sarcasm or menace it said, 'Do not be afraid.'

But Lazarus was. And very.

With no warning the figure dropped Lazarus to the ground, but didn't let go its grip. It started to drag him away from the Defender.

Lazarus spun like a spindle to try to dislodge himself and rip away from the vice-like hand. His feet and legs were dragging through muck and mire, drenching him in freezing mud and water and he was soon shivering, though perhaps out of fear more than the cold. The only moment of reprieve was when he was dragged over Abaddon's still body, which Lazarus hadn't seen move once since waking from the crash. He yelled out and kicked hard, but Abaddon didn't stir.

'You are a fighter, Lazarus, that I will acknowledge.'

The voice was hypnotic, entrancing, and Lazarus had little choice but to listen.

'But resistance is futile now. I am sure you can appreciate that, yes?'

'What do you want?' Lazarus gasped, now out of breath from his struggling. 'Who were those two people on the motorbike? How did you find us?'

A laugh came next, and to Lazarus it sounded like music, but played on a piano smashed and broken.

'Have you ever studied the food chain, Lazarus?'

A science quiz? What the . . . ?

'What's the food chain got to do with anything?'

'Everything is about to change, Lazarus. The Dead will see to that. As will we. And humanity will slip a few links, if you catch my meaning.'

'I don't,' said Lazarus, trying again to spin free, but his knees cracked against a stone and a ripple of pain raced through his nerves. 'And what do you mean by "we"? What the hell are you?'

The figure stopped. For a moment, the only sensation Lazarus felt, other than the cold creeping up his legs from his ice cube feet, was of a pulse in the hand holding him. The next was being pulled up face-to-face to stare into eyes that swirled like a galaxy of stars being sucked into a black hole.

'We were your beginning, and now we are your very end, sweet Lazarus.'

As the sound of his name was swallowed by the wind, Lazarus was launched skyward to land in a pool of mucky, stinking bog an impossible distance from the figure. He could still see the Defender and the figure standing between him and it, but there was still no sign of a rescue mission from Abaddon or Arielle. He was alone in this. And about to die, of that he had no doubt.

With the figure's last words waltzing around in his head, Lazarus tried to move, pull himself out of the bog and give himself a chance at escape. But something was wrong; he couldn't move, couldn't budge. He tried again, pulled every ounce of survival instinct he had into moving his legs, getting himself up and out, but nothing. Fear reached in and squeezed his heart as it raced in panic; he was paralysed. Lazarus didn't know if it was because he'd landed badly, or because of something the figure had done, but it didn't matter; he couldn't move, had lost all sensation from the neck down. And just when he thought it couldn't get any worse, that he was about to be sent from this world into the next in a no doubt horribly painful and violent way, he saw movement by the Defender. But the brief moment of hope that Arielle was coming soon dissolved as, from the thick shadows under the vehicle's wheels, Lazarus saw terror claw its way out and start to make its slow, painful, path across the moor towards him.

And the voice of the creature quietly whispered, 'Game over . . .'

4

MUTILATED BODIES

Their faces were crushed beyond recognition. And what was left of the rest of them bore little if any resemblance to the humans they had once been. The sight of them brought with it such a crippling, fetid stink of death, which forced its way into his nose, his mouth, down his throat, that despite now being able to control his reaction to it, Lazarus heaved and gobbed out a trickle of hot vomit. It slipped down his cheek to pool in his ear.

Lazarus panicked. 'Abaddon! Arielle! For god's sake, wake up and help!' But the only response was that of the rain spattering the murky water around him into tiny black crowns.

Lazarus refused to accept that he was completely helpless. He'd been in situations this bad before, and he'd pulled through, survived. But here something was different. The things slipping and sliding towards him only added to that sense of utter helplessness.

Being run over by a Defender was going to do some damage, but to see it for real, squirming closer and closer, made Lazarus's flesh crawl like bugs had got under his skin and were burrowing deeper, scurrying through his veins, working their way to the thick red warmth deep inside.

The figure on the left, the one who'd been up front on the motorcycle, was missing most of the left side of his face and head, the remnants nothing more than bloody wet ribbons whipped into a tangle. Both legs were gone just above the knee, and its chest had been squashed so dreadfully that his guts had burst out through splits in his sides. The other, the passenger, had no legs at all; just odd, mashed strands of blood and bone that looked like the ruined tentacles of a giant squid. That its arms were able to function in any away at all, and pull it forwards, was a miracle, as both had lost most of their flesh and muscle. A gleam of bone was visible in so many places, and the torso's face was smashed so badly that all Lazarus could make out were the teeth; and they seemed to grin and chatter at him like a wind-up toy. The rattling, clattering sound they made was like they were getting in a last minute bit of practice for what he guessed they were soon about to do.

The naked figure walked forward, each step offered with precision. It knelt down and brushed away some dirt and mulch from his face, then used some torn grass to wipe away the vomit from his mouth and ear. Lazarus shivered at the touch; that an act so caring could be so cold and foul gored him. Again he tried to move. Again he was utterly helpless.

'You cannot escape, Lazarus.' The figure's breath was perfumed like the scent of fresh-cut flowers. 'And although it will eventually be over, I cannot really say that it will be over soon. You will suffer. As must we all. In suffering do we not in the end find true peace?'

Lazarus ignored the psycho religious babble coming from the figure. He guessed asking it questions about who it was and what it was doing would at best encourage it. But then he had already guessed where it was from, hadn't he? And there was only one place that could possibly be, somewhere impossible to escape from, somewhere guarded for eternity: Hell!

Pushing away that thought, Lazarus ignored the chill it gave his blood and the ice it brought to the very air he breathed. The crushed, mutilated bodies were only a spit away now, and in the eyes of them both he saw something a little more pressing than Hell returning; it was that same lust he'd seen in all of the Dead. Only this time it wasn't about the simple stolen chance to experience life again in the body of a living, breathing person. No, this was more primitive and spoke of a hunger that would only be sated by something eaten. And that something, he knew from the very bottom of his sickened stomach, was him.

The figure stood up to stare down at Lazarus, an impossible and improbable look of compassion on its face.

A whimpering cry, like that of a wounded animal, escaped Lazarus's lips. 'Please, don't leave me here! You can't!'

As the last word died, something pulled at his legs. For a moment, Lazarus thought it was just the hands of the dead things that had crawled to him, using him to pull themselves further up. But as it continued, he quickly realised that they weren't moving at all. And that the pulling wasn't of hands, but of teeth, shredding his clothes, shredding his flesh. But there was no pain at all. Being paralysed, he thought darkly, had its advantages.

The figure looked for a moment to where the torsos were now gnawing at Lazarus, gave him a final glance, then turned and walked away.

'You can't leave me!' yelled Lazarus, his body tugged more and more vigorously. 'You can't! You hear me? I can't die here! Not like this! I'm the bloody Keeper! My dad . . .'

Lazarus could think of nothing more to say and his head sank back into thick, cold mud. Above him the sky was a swirling soup of black and grey. Rain was still falling, washing his face, slipping into his nose and mouth. And at his feet, the awful remains of two people he'd run over were ripping into him with their teeth, the sound of chewing horribly clear in the buzz and clamour of the storm.

Tears took over. They flooded out of Lazarus like rivers

bursting their banks. And he yelled out more in anger than pain.

All this, and for what? Why had he ever thought he could do anything but fail? He'd tried to get his dad back, save him from what the Dead were doing to him, would use him for, but not only had he screwed that up, he'd gone and lost two others in the process. Dying here was all he deserved. And it was all he was going to get.

The figure moved further away into the shifting shadows of the wet black night. He wanted to call it back, strike a bargain, but knew it was useless. So he continued to stare and, in the final moments before the figure faded completely into the gloom, saw two things that nailed him to the ground. First was the flash of vast wings splayed out and dusted in moonlight. The second was that the creature was now clearly male.

As those impossible wings slipped from view into the grim darkness lying all around, feeling returned to Lazarus's body. The pain of what was being done to his feet, his legs, burned through him like a welding torch on butter, and he did the only thing left to him; he screamed. And it pulled with it the agony not just of where the pain was coming from, but of his whole body being so terribly abused.

Lazarus felt every bite, every tug, every rip, every tear. And the searing pain reached such a pitch that he wondered why he wasn't just passing out, because that was all he wanted to do now, to be taken somewhere else, where none of this would bother him and he could finally give up.

Letting out yet another screeching yell, Lazarus saw something move over by the Defender. He squeezed his eyes into narrow slits to focus better through the rain. The rear door of the truck dropped open and Arielle fell out and on to the ground on her back.

Lazarus forced out a piercing yell so loud it felt like it was shredding his lungs. 'Arielle! ARIELLE!'

For a second that lasted for ever, nothing happened. Arielle was still on the ground. She wasn't moving. Then, almost as though it was in reply to his own anguished cry, Arielle roared, was on her feet, and running.

5
GNAWED BONES, BLOOD AND GRISTLE

Lazarus caught the flash of Arielle's sword as she ripped it from its scabbard, then closed the gap between them in a single leap. The figure appeared once again, this time its wings clear for all to see, its hair no longer bloody, but silvery white, untouched by blood or rain. Its once calm face was no longer serene, but pulled into an animal snarl of teeth and death.

'Behind you!' rasped Lazarus, his voice little more than a desperate, pained breath.

Arielle turned and something like recognition passed between her and the winged figure.

Its voice rang out clear and pure as a newly cast church bell. 'Will you not ever die, angel?'

'Not today!' challenged Arielle, her eyes narrow like a

prowling cat. 'And not for you!'

The figure snarled, and the sound of it rumbled and tumbled round the hills like the roar from a tiger denied its kill. Then it was gone.

Arielle snapped her head round to Lazarus and brought her sword to bear in two swift, deadly arcs. With each she cut the gnawing torsos away from Lazarus, severing their arms, and then hoofed them hard to land with a damp splat in a pool of mud writhing in the rain like it was filled with maggots. The things were not yet completely finished, and as Arielle knelt down to help Lazarus sit up, they desperately tried to pull themselves back to him on bloody stumps, even using their mouths to gain some purchase on the grass.

Lazarus knew his injuries were bad by the look scratched into Arielle's face.

'I should've been more careful,' she whispered. 'Sensed something was going to happen . . .'

Hot pain burned like molten lead through Lazarus.

'I can't move,' he said. 'Whatever that thing was, it paralysed me.'

'Can you feel anything?'

'That a trick question?'

Arielle didn't even flicker a smile. 'Your injuries, Lazarus . . .' She paused, then said, 'Look for yourself.'

Lazarus stared at what was left of his feet and legs. They were nothing but gnawed bones, blood and gristle. Even the crippling pain wasn't enough to convince him they were his.

'They'll heal, right? I mean, I'm the Keeper. I've got that special angel healing power, haven't I?'

Lazarus wanted to smile. Couldn't.

Arielle's face was grave. 'Your legs are a mess, your feet gone. There's nothing left except a few bones and some ligaments and flesh holding them together.'

The pain was being slowly replaced by an odd, tingling sensation.

'You don't sound too positive.'

'Healing has to be done within reason, have something to work with, but . . . you're a mess!'

Arielle had stopped speaking because in that same moment she'd seen the same as Lazarus; the slow recovery of flesh and skin to a small section of his left foot. It was pink and perfect and new. In other places other small areas of new skin could be seen.

'They're healing, Lazarus!' said Arielle, clearly astonished.

Lazarus winced. 'Bloody stings though!'

A movement caught Lazarus's attention. The torsos were still thrashing in the mud.

'You going to leave them there or what?'

Arielle stood up and sauntered over to the torsos. They were now almost completely covered in thick, brown mud.

She reached inside her jacket and pulled out the same revolver she'd used to shoot Lazarus when they first met. One of the torsos glanced up at her only to find the barrel shoved into its mouth. When Arielle pulled the trigger, the back of its head momentarily transformed itself into a bright, pink cloud, before it slumped forwards to sink beneath the mud. The other torso, utterly oblivious to what had happened, didn't register at all as Arielle raise her boot, then brought it down to crush its skull completely with the sound of a coconut being hit by a hammer. Then it too slipped slowly back into the mud.

'You're certainly thorough,' said Lazarus as Arielle

walked back towards him.

Arielle holstered her pistol. 'It's a girl thing,' she said, then squatted down and slipped her arms round Lazarus's back and under his knees. Her muscles tensed and he was hoisted upwards. Arielle started to walk back towards the Defender.

'And for a girl, you're strong.'

'For a boy, you talk a lot.'

'So you going to tell me what that was? Or do I have to guess?'

Arielle ignored the question, slowed her pace a little, and nodded over to Abaddon's still body on the ground. 'Has he moved since the crash?'

Lazarus shook his head. 'I was heading out to check him when that thing turned up and ripped the door off the Defender and dragged me over here. Which brings me nicely back to my original question.'

'I didn't get a good look at it,' said Arielle, sounding guarded.

'Well, I did,' said Lazarus. 'It was huge, probably three metres tall. Its skin was badly damaged, but healed up quicker than you or me. Except for the hair on its head, it was bald *everywhere*. Smooth, like plastic.'

'That's not so unusual,' said Arielle.

'You want to know the really freaky thing?'

Arielle said nothing. Lazarus just continued anyway.

'When I first saw it, it had no sexual organs, right? Nothing! I mean, it was completely blank. Later? Right as it was leaving? It was male! What's all that about, Arielle? What kind of creature is able to decide what sex it wants to be?'

Still with the silence.

'Talk to me, Arielle. I'm the Keeper, you're my guardian, so you pretty much have to do what I say!'

Arielle flinched.

'If I'm to meet any more of whatever the hell that was,' said Lazarus, 'don't you think it would be a good idea to tell me what it is? Give me a few pointers as to how to take the thing down if I meet it again? Particularly as it'll probably be in the village we're heading to, remember? The one so nicely situated in Hell?'

Arielle stopped walking. A few paces away lay Abaddon.

'Look, Lazarus,' she began, her voice faltering.

Whatever she was about to tell him, it was seriously bothering her. 'That creature you saw? It's not one of the Dead.'

'I know. There was no smell on it. It was from Hell, right?'

Arielle's mouth fell open at just the same moment as Abaddon stirred from his slumber.

'We'll discuss this later,' said Arielle, covering the last few steps to Abaddon.

'You've got that right,' Lazarus replied under his breath.

Abaddon rose to his feet like he was attached to strings and a puppet master was pulling him up from the ground. He glanced around then looked to Arielle and Lazarus.

'You missed all the fun,' said Lazarus before Abaddon had a chance to speak.

'I remember the crash,' said Abaddon. 'After that, nothing.'

'Convenient,' said Lazarus.

'Not convenient,' Abaddon growled. 'Impossible.'

'How do you mean?'

Abaddon bent down to pick up his hat. 'I cannot be

rendered unconscious, Lazarus. I am dead. My body does not rest.'

'You were asleep when I was driving,' said Lazarus. 'You said you were dreaming!'

'I rest out of choice,' Abaddon replied. 'I let my mind wander where it wants. But to be physically unconscious? It has never happened before.'

'Not quite true,' said Arielle. 'It's happened *once* before – remember?'

Abaddon clearly didn't like being reminded of that memory. He scowled at Arielle with such venom Lazarus thought he was going to attack her.

'You tricked me, angel,' he muttered. 'Then you suffocated an echo of life inside me just enough to render me unable to retaliate.'

Lazarus hadn't a clue what either of them were talking about and he wasn't about to be left out of the conversation. Not least because what he'd just heard had made sense of something else. It confirmed what he'd been thinking all along.

'So the last time you were unconscious was because of Arielle?'

Abaddon nodded. 'No matter what you may have heard, never trust an angel, Lazarus, never.'

When Lazarus then looked into Arielle's eyes he saw in them not just the knowledge that he'd guessed about the huge figure with the wings, but a sorrow deep enough to drown in.

'So it *was* an angel,' he said. 'Like you!'

Arielle nodded. 'And an angel from a place where those who were sent were never supposed to be able to escape. Until now.'

At this, Abaddon drew close. 'A Fallen One was here? Then we must away to the village! Now!'

Arielle agreed.

'You know what this means?' said Abaddon.

'That we are not simply dealing with the Dead returning,' said Arielle. 'Yeah, I know.'

'Then you also know, angel, that from this point on, what we face is more than any of us, even working together, have any chance of overcoming!'

'We have no choice!' Arielle snapped back. 'Whatever is coming is coming, and we must do what we must do. We have run out of options! At least we have the Keeper!'

'And they have his father!' snapped Abaddon, before turning to walk back to the Defender.

Arielle followed carrying Lazarus as though he were no weight at all. When they arrived at the vehicle, Arielle rested Lazarus in the back. She pulled a bottle of wine from a cubby hole under the seat and chugging the liquid down, checked the damage. Although the engine was running fine, and the body work was pretty roughed up in places, torn away completely in others, their real problem was tyres; the front ones were shredded beyond repair, and she had only one spare. That and the small issue of no windscreen.

'So you're not a member of the AA,' said Lazarus. 'And I'm not talking about the car rescue service.'

Arielle sunk another glug.

'Like I said, you drink too much.'

'Wrong,' said Arielle, wiping her mouth free of dribble. 'I don't drink enough.'

Lazarus stared at the Defender. It looked dead. 'So why can't you just fly us to where we're going?' he asked. 'In fact, why haven't you just flown us all the way here?'

'It's not as easy as you think,' said Arielle, casting a look that said shut the hell up.

Lazarus was trying to think of something else to say, if only to keep Arielle focused on thinking up a solution, when from somewhere in the darkness blanketing the moors came the sound of a rattling, clattering engine.

'You hear that?'

Arielle nodded, dropped the now empty wine bottle to the floor, stepped out of the rear of the Defender, and stared into the darkness. And out of it emerged a battered old tractor towing a trailer.

It stopped, and from the rusting cab stepped a man in an overcoat, wellies and a woollen hat.

'Let me guess,' he said, looking at each of them in turn. 'More hippies looking for the festival, right?'

7
NO ESCAPE

Lazarus wasn't too sure about the dog sitting in the trailer. It was a huge beast and kept licking its lips when it looked up at him.

'Does it bite?'

The farmer laughed as he helped Arielle and Abaddon up into the trailer.

'What, old Jack there? He's an old softy! Doesn't even bother to fetch rabbits for me now, do you, lad?'

Despite it being the middle of the night, Abaddon was wearing a pair of sunglasses from Arielle. He'd resisted at first, but she'd had a point; meeting someone with no eyes would freak anyone out. They didn't need any extra attention.

Jack's tail wagged. It sounded like a thick lump of rope thwacking the trailer floor hard enough to crack it.

'How far did he say the farm was?' Lazarus asked Arielle.

'Couple of miles. He's giving us somewhere to rest for the night out of the rain. We'll fix the Defender tomorrow. He's got a spare tyre we can have.'

Abaddon slumped down. 'I do not like this.'

'Beats waiting the night out in the rain, don't you think?' replied Arielle.

'I do not feel the rain. I do not feel the cold,' rumbled Abaddon. Then added, 'I feel nothing.'

The journey didn't take long and Lazarus huddled down as best he could against the cold, pulling Arielle's jacket in tight. The rain drumming a tattoo around him, he closed his eyes and let himself drift a little. The emotions he'd felt in the presence of that angel rushed at him again. The sense that he'd failed his dad had been overwhelming. The weight of the responsibility of what he had to do pushed down on him and made him short of breath. What scared him the most wasn't just the thought that he could still fail, that his father could still be out of reach, but that worse was to come.

The tractor pulled into a farmyard and juddered to a halt outside a tired house. Inside, it was basic but cosy, thanks to an old wood-burning stove.

The farmer left them to get warm, placing a battered kettle on the stove before heading out to check on some livestock. Jack stayed with them, hunched up between the stove and Lazarus's feet.

'A good man,' said Arielle. 'We're lucky he found us.'

Lazarus sensed luck had nothing to do with it. He had little idea of the true power of an angel; for all he knew, she could have sent for him.

'I didn't catch his name.'

'Willie,' said Arielle. 'He's a widower; runs this place by himself now. Not an easy life by any stretch of the imagination.'

Abaddon was statue-still by the stove.

'So what's it like being dead?' asked Lazarus.

'I can't remember,' said Abaddon.

'But you're dead now.'

'Yes and no. I am still here, this is still my body, but I feel like a tenant more than an owner.'

Willie walked back in. 'I've found you a spare tyre for

the morning. Shouldn't take long to fix you up and have you on your way.'

Lazarus remembered what Willie had said to them when he'd met them on the hill. 'So what's this festival then?' he asked. 'Sort of like Glastonbury?'

'Hippies,' Willie replied. 'Bloody thousands of the buggers blocking up the roads with their knackered camper vans!'

'Where is it? I didn't see anything that looked like a festival on our way here.'

Willie walked over to a window set deep in the thick wall opposite the front door. He tapped the glass.

'Down there,' he said. 'Side of the lake. The land was bought by this rich git, James Barton, a city bloke who wanted a slice of country pie!'

'And he runs it?'

Willie nodded. 'There's a religious commune on the other side of the lake. Used to be just a few holiday cabins round an old church ruin. He set it up for people who want to find themselves, if you know what I mean.'

Lazarus knew what Willie was getting at: tree-hugging vegetarians and UFO spotters.

'He comes on a holiday, has an epiphany down by the lake, and next thing he's living like John the Baptist in a Range Rover, has bought the holiday cabins, and before we know what's happening we've this festival on our doorstep!'

Abaddon joined Willie at the window, his forehead close enough to touch the glass.

'I see it,' he said, his voice like tumbling boulders. 'It has a name.'

Lazarus was struck by the way Abaddon said those last four words; not a question, a statement.

'Lake Semmerwater,' said Willie.

Abaddon turned from the window and stared hard at Arielle.

'Let me guess,' she said. 'Home, right?'

The next morning, an early start had brought them all back to the Defender with the day still breaking. Willie had fixed the truck and accepted payment for the damage to the wall. Now Arielle was in the driving seat and keen to get going.

'Lazarus – in! Abaddon?' called Arielle.

Lazarus, in boots Willie had given him to replace the ones he'd lost the night before, looked over at the dead priest standing alone a few metres away from the vehicle. He'd not said a word to anyone that morning. Lazarus was unnerved by his silence.

'Funny old bugger, isn't he?' said Willie as Lazarus climbed into the rear of the Defender. 'Hell of a tan on him too. Can't be good for you, can it, all that sunbed stuff? And does he always wear sunglasses?'

Abaddon walked over to them, like a lost spectre looking for somewhere to haunt, slipping into the passenger seat with little more than a nod of acknowledgement.

Willie stood back to allow Arielle to edge forward and back round to the road.

'Thanks again, Willie,' she smiled, leaning out through the window.

Lazarus thanked Willie for the boots. They weren't exactly his kind of thing, but he had a feeling that the steel toecaps would come in useful pretty soon.

Willie waved as the Defender crunched up the road. 'You all remember to pop in if you're ever this way again; door's always open!'

Arielle and Lazarus waved as Willie disappeared behind them. Lazarus wasn't sure he was going to survive the next few days, never mind long enough to come back for a weekend break.

Abaddon remained motionless, like his batteries had run down. That was until the Defender crested the top of the hill and started to wind a way down the road towards the lake, to join a thick vein of traffic pulsing with music, and squealing brakes. The traffic was all heading to one place: the festival.

Abaddon broke his silence. 'With the Fallen involved, finding the village is more important than ever.'

'You're getting repetitive,' sighed Lazarus.

'What lies there is the reason you were sent to find me, boy!'

'The village?'

Arielle butted in. 'Abaddon's right. With the Fallen involved, we have to stop this getting any worse before we find ourselves unable to do anything to stop them!'

Abaddon's neck creaked as he shifted round, removed his sunglasses and stared at Lazarus. Those hollow sockets made Lazarus wish he'd put them right back on again.

'I have not told you everything, Lazarus.'

Lazarus knew he wasn't going to like what he was about to hear. Outside the road, like a thin grey snake, slithered down the valley to Lake Semmerwater, which looked like a hole in the world. And they were falling into it.

'I bet there's plenty you haven't told me,' he said. 'And I'm happy for it to stay like that if it's all the same with you.'

Abaddon ignored him. 'When my village turned against me, they didn't have to listen to the lies, but they were weak, many gave in.'

Lazarus sensed the end of the story was going to be one he didn't want to hear.

'They paid a price.'

'Because of what they did,' said Lazarus, growing tired of Abaddon always labouring the point. 'I get it!'

Abaddon was unmoved. 'When I stepped back into this world, a walking corpse, the village was changed beyond all recognition. Those with families had left. It was a childless place, the joy sucked out of it.'

'Doesn't sound like much of a holiday destination.'

'The place stank of evil. It was everywhere; in the

brickwork of the houses, on the breath of the people, in the rain that washed the muck away from the cobbles of the roads.'

'Is this where I'm supposed to ask what happened?'

'It was I who cast the place into Hell, Lazarus! Red played his part, but it was my call. I was warned of the consequences, but I ripped open the veil and sent them crashing to damnation! And being dead gave me a unique perspective on what I had done, trust me.'

This was news to Lazarus. The veil was the barrier that lay between this world and the next, and between that and Hell. He'd seen it open, had been told that as the Keeper he had the power to do such a thing himself. But Abaddon had opened it too?

'I don't understand. How did you open the veil?'

Abaddon stared into the middle distance, like he was reliving a memory. 'I stepped into that lake, curious to see what I had done. If Hell ever needed a weakness to exploit, I had given it one; a loose brick in the wall that surrounded it.'

Lazarus was growing tired of Abaddon's riddles. 'Get to the sodding point!'

'Send that many people to Hell at once,' said Abaddon, his voice like approaching thunder, 'an entire village, the buildings, the very land it is built on, and it leaves a scar. The village is in Hell, Lazarus! It lies in the distant, endless black lands that surround it, and out of reach of the terrible, burning reality of that place.'

Lazarus could tell Abaddon wasn't telling him everything. It was hidden in those last few words about the reality of Hell.

Abaddon jabbed a pointed finger downwards, as if emphasising just how close the village was.

'But the village . . . it is also here! A shadow of it remains, trapped between both worlds, an ever-bleeding wound between the world of the Living and that of the Dead!'

Lazarus shook his head, screwed up his face, as though the information he was being given tasted as bad as it sounded. And the mention of Red just added to the confusion. What Red was, he still wasn't sure, but he had appeared in his life a few days ago and started all this. How he'd looked had burned into Lazarus's mind; a body stripped of its skin, demanding to see his dad, talking about the Dead slipping through to this world. Was Red an angel? Didn't matter. It was his arrival that had turned Lazarus's world upside down, and sent him spinning into a darkness he wondered if he'd ever escape from.

'So what you're saying is that because of what you and Red did to this village, Hell can blast through to our world and go on the rampage?'

Abaddon fell into a silence that sucked all sound from the moment and crushed it to nothing.

Lazarus wasn't backing off because, no matter how big and black the full picture was, at its centre lay his dad and his friends. 'If what you've just said is true, then how the living crap is visiting this village in any way going to help us now? And what has this to do with Dad?'

He didn't care that he sounded angry. Just when things seemed to make a little sense, something would come along and shatter it like a boulder smashed on to a beetle's back.

Abaddon nodded to Arielle. She pulled the Defender out of the slow-moving traffic and drove them into a parking area that looked out across the lake. About a mile away to their left, people were flooding into the fields for the festival. Just a few metres away from the front of the Defender, the lake lapped a pebbled shore. Sunlight shimmered on its surface but seemed to have to fight to stay alive, like each wave was trying to extinguish it.

What Abaddon did next would scar Lazarus's mind for the rest of his life.

8

THICK FOLDS OF FLESH

Abaddon removed his jacket and shirt to reveal a corpse's skin as deep a brown as a slick of thick gravy, and as tough as elephant hide. It was almost impossible to find a section of it that wasn't scarred and cut with gashes somehow fused back together. In the deeper cuts, black thread could be seen stitching one side to the other. But most hideous of all was the huge wound stretching from Abaddon's chest to his navel. And down its full length the whole thing was held together by a thick stretch of black leather cord.

Lazarus went to say something, but Arielle shook her head. He clamped his mouth shut. He noticed then that she looked as intrigued as he was himself; had she no idea either what Abaddon was about to do either?

Abaddon reached into his jacket and removed a

knife. It was small, with a thin blade that folded out of a white bone handle. The blade looked like it would cut through flesh with the ease of a butcher's knife through soft pig fat. Abaddon slipped the blade under the first of the thick stitches holding his chest together. And cut it open.

Lazarus gasped. 'What the hell are you doing? You can't just open yourself up! You'll die!'

The idiocy of what he'd said struck him hard, but surely something bad would happen; even if you're dead, opening up your own chest couldn't be a good thing.

Abaddon wasn't listening and, with slow precision, cut each and every stitch in his chest. He folded the knife and slipped it back into his jacket with a little bit of affection.

The look Abaddon then gave Lazarus was that of a man who was not only willing to do anything to get the job done, but had already done so. He had travelled paths darker than any nightmare could imagine. Lazarus knew he could do nothing about the fact that he was about to follow him down another.

Abaddon rested his hands on either side of the now stitchless wound. Then he forced his fingers into it, pushing them between the thick folds of flesh, and pulled himself apart.

Lazarus held a hand to his mouth in shock, pinned to the moment by the very stitches he'd just seen Abaddon remove. He glanced at Arielle and she too was glued to what was unfolding in front of them.

'It can't be . . .' she said, and Lazarus wasn't happy that she sounded like she knew what was about to happen next. 'You and Red, you both promised!'

At the mention of Red again, Lazarus's skin tingled. He didn't want to meet that creature again, not ever. But what he did or didn't want had nothing to do with it; his world had spun out of control then exploded into a thousand shards of night.

Abaddon reached deep inside the open wound with his left hand. His face betrayed no reaction to what he was doing, no discomfort, no pain. It looked like his chest was eating his hand, slowly chewing its way up his arm as he pushed it further inside. When Abaddon pulled his hand back out, it was covered with a substance as black and thick as tar, which released the faint smell of rotting leaves, like the last moments of autumn before winter finally kills it off. And held in its grasp was something wrapped in a greasy cloth.

At this, Lazarus saw the look on Arielle's face turn from mild confusion and intrigue, to one of utter shock, then finally bitter rage.

'It's impossible,' she gasped, her voice breaking, almost unable to bridge the gap between the words. 'You said it was destroyed! You lied to me! I should never have left you in that cave! I should have sent you to the other side for good when I had the chance!'

'I know,' said Abaddon the slime-covered thing resting in his hands like a newborn baby. 'But this . . . it gave me that edge I needed, angel. Why else do you think the Dead were always so afraid of me? And you always suspected something, did you not? And Red's involvement.'

'I should never have believed you,' Arielle replied, her eyes narrowing. 'Yes, I always had my suspicions. I just never acted on them.'

'Your naturally suspicious nature is one of your strengths,' smiled Abaddon, 'and something that makes you equally infuriating.'

'And with good reason, it seems.'

Abaddon reached out a hand. 'A towel, Lazarus.'

Abaddon wiped the thing he'd pulled from his chest cavity, and his hands, then handed it to Arielle. She unwrapped it carefully, almost like she was afraid it would explode or shatter, and eventually Lazarus saw what Abaddon had kept hidden inside himself. It was a shard of black stone, a hand's span in length, and it rested in Arielle's grip with a weight that seemed to be pulling the world into it like a magnet. Lazarus could see strange markings down one side of the piece of rock, etched into what was clearly a smoother edge than the rest.

'Your chest,' said Lazarus, unable to tear his eyes away from the leaking cavity. 'Shouldn't we repair it?'

Abaddon shook his head with deliberate slowness.

Lazarus was finding sitting in front of a speaking corpse with its chest ripped open a little distracting. It didn't help that the wound was leaking and that the towel, which Abaddon had placed at the base of the wound on his lap, was slowly darkening with a stain from the black liquid weeping from it.

'This, Lazarus,' Abaddon said, nodding at the thing

now unwrapped and lying in Arielle's hands, 'is why Red sent you to find me. With your father's disappearance, he knew this was all connected. It is why the Dead always feared me, why everything is racing towards the one moment I have always known would eventually come. A reckoning, Lazarus, unlike anything the world has ever witnessed. And perhaps my own story's end.'

'It should have been destroyed,' said Arielle, repeating herself with a whisper, shaking her head like she was trying to dislodge the thought for good.

'You think I do not know that?' Abaddon replied harshly. 'But—'

'In this there are no buts!' snapped Arielle and Lazarus was shocked to hear her sudden anger. 'You know what this is, don't you, Abaddon? Yes, it gave you an edge, but it being here has kept a faint thread intact, one you could have severed a long time ago and saved us all a lot of trouble! It's acted like a bloody homing signal to Hell, and guess what? Hell has heard and it's coming! THEY'RE coming; the FALLEN!'

Lazarus knew things were kicking off and reached out to touch the stone, but Abaddon shook his head at the same time as Arielle reached out to prevent his hand getting any closer.

'But it's just a lump of rock,' said Lazarus. 'What's it got to do with anything that's been going on?'

'This,' explained Arielle, her voice like it was drowning in fear, 'is the Black Shard. And it is not of this world.'

'You could teach lessons on how to make things sound ominous,' said Lazarus.

'How it came to be here at all is unknown,' continued Abaddon, with the voice of an adult explaining something very important to a young child. 'But its origins lie—'

'In Hell, right?' Lazarus cut in, knowing he'd guessed correctly, but wishing he hadn't. 'That place seems to be featuring pretty heavily in everything we're saying or doing.'

Abaddon and Arielle nodded together.

'I first saw the stone the night my family were murdered,' said Abaddon, his body seeming to almost sink a little with the memory of what he was saying. 'It was used to open up a rip between this world and that which lies beyond. I saw something crawl out through that rip, Lazarus. And it took . . .'

Abaddon's voice broke on his words, like getting over them would tear him apart. He clenched his fists. When he spoke again, his voice was strong.

'It took my daughter, Mary. She was but seven years old! My wife and my son had been murdered in front of me only moments before. That night was the last I ever saw her. It changed . . . everything.'

It was the first time Lazarus had heard any emotion in Abaddon's voice other than anger. The sorrow of those last words drenched him. Whatever Abaddon had witnessed that night had made him what he was now. And the unutterable horror of it was unimaginable.

'How did you get hold of it? Why?'

Abaddon fell silent.

Lazarus looked to Arielle for answers.

'Like Abaddon said, that night changed him,' she said. 'What was done . . . what he witnessed? No one could ever have foreseen what it would set in motion.'

'I became vengeance and retribution, Lazarus,' said Abaddon. 'They murdered me. So when I came back I didn't just kill, I ripped information from them as they screamed for me to stop! And I kept on ripping, even in death, following them through the veil, never letting go, never stopping! They hoped for death, for the release it would bring, but it brought none. Not with me at their side. And not with the Black Shard inside me!'

'You tortured them!' hissed Arielle, unable to disguise her disgust. 'And don't give me all that means-justifies-the-ends shit! They murdered your family, and what you did to them put you on their level! Perhaps even below it!'

Abaddon ignored her, shaking his head slightly, like he'd heard it all before, and wasn't interested in listening. He held up a hand to shush Arielle.

'In death I found Red. I told him of the stone. We made a deal; he would give me the chance for vengeance and I would retrieve the Black Shard.'

'So what does it do?' asked Lazarus, annoyed yet again of Abaddon's ability to cloud his explanations with waffle.

'Without the Black Shard,' said Abaddon, his voice in that moment like the faint ripple on the surface of a still lake at night-time, 'I would be terrible, yes, but still vulnerable. Yet with it, I could not only last for centuries, but its dark power would run through me; it gave me the ability that you and Arielle have to sense the Dead, sniff them out, hunt them down. And I could walk between worlds, follow the Dead, take the fight to them!'

Abaddon reached into the air between them with his right hand, and took the Black Shard from Arielle in his left. If he'd had eyes, thought Lazarus, they would have looked wild.

'I could pull them from the living body they had occupied and send them back to where they came from! And if it was too late, if there was no hope for the body, I could kill!'

Sparks crackled at the tips of Abaddon's fingers. A thin crack appeared in the air between his hands, and as it opened the stench of death slipped out.

9
DRIED SPLATTERS OF BLOOD

Lazarus retched. For the briefest moment his head swam, then he got it under control and locked it away.

Arielle moved too quickly for Abaddon or Lazarus to respond, bringing her revolver out to pinch the ancient flesh of Abaddon's face with the muzzle of the barrel. She clicked the hammer back slowly, deliberately.

'Your weapon cannot harm me, angel.'

'No, but it can seriously screw up your next hat fitting,' said Arielle. 'Do not do that here!'

The sparks fizzled out, the crack disappeared, the smell vanished.

'I was and am the Dead's executioner,' said Abaddon, slipping the stone back inside his chest, as Arielle eased the hammer back on the revolver and lowered it. 'And I work for Red, the jailer of Hell. I give no second chances.'

'And that is why we had to stop him,' said Arielle, turning to Lazarus. Then she used the barrel of her revolver to point at Abaddon, jabbing it at him to emphasise her anger. 'He had no right to do what he was doing, even with Red's involvement! It was not his place! I have always wondered how he had the power to do what he did. I should have guessed it was the Black Shard! I was a fool!'

Arielle threw her hands in the air in obvious frustration then stowed the revolver and rested her head on the steering wheel.

'But there is more, angel.'

Arielle sat up slowly and Lazarus felt as though the world was listening in.

'What else haven't you told me?' asked Arielle.

Abaddon looked down at the grey waters of the lake. 'To send the village to Hell I needed something that would keep it there, nail it to the foundations of that dreadful place.'

'I don't understand . . .'

Abaddon once again reached into his jacket and pulled out a roll of the cord that had held him together.

'I always carry a spare,' he said, and began to thread it through the holes in his dead flesh. 'The Black Shard, Arielle. It was the only thing capable of keeping the village in Hell.'

Arielle's brow crease with concern. 'What did you do?'

'I broke it in two; half for me, half to pin the village down.'

'You can't be serious!'

Abaddon cut in. 'The village is kept in Hell through the power of the Black Shard, Arielle. I buried the other half in the grave of my wife and son . . .'

Arielle screamed, back-handing Abaddon with such force he bashed his head against the door. He did not respond in kind.

'You bloody idiot!'

'I did not know what trouble it would cause.' His voice was hollow, sad almost, and Lazarus actually believed him. 'This could not have been foreseen, that it would weaken the veil. So now I must find it and destroy it!'

Abaddon tied off the end of the cord, pulled his shirt closed and the wound was again hidden from sight.

'Sounds like the first good idea any of us have had,' said Lazarus. 'Except that the other half is in a village that's either at the bottom of a lake or in Hell or both!'

'I will go,' said Abaddon. 'You, Keeper, cannot. With the Black Shard destroyed, the weakness in the veil will fade. Even with the power of the Dark at their disposal, they will be unable to bring all of Hell through to this world. And we will have a chance, at least.'

Lazarus looked over at Arielle. Her shoulders had slumped under the weight of what Abaddon had said. His mind burst with a thousand questions, but he ignored them, and instead focused on where they were and what they were about to do.

'If the veil has always been weak here,' he said, feeling the almost physical sensation of events clicking into place, 'then the Dead have always been able to slip through, right? So why has no one ever noticed? How has this place remained so secret?'

'We don't know that the Dead have being doing that,' said Arielle. 'It's not that simple.'

Lazarus wasn't so sure. 'Everything has been building to this, hasn't it? The Dead, Mum tricking Dad through the veil to become the Dark, Red having no choice but to send us to Abaddon, the Black Shard . . .'

Arielle said nothing. Abaddon was dead.

Lazarus, more lost and frustrated than ever before, stared out across the lake in front of them. A thought bled into his mind; if the Black Shard was destroyed, what then would become of Abaddon?

The valley outside the Defender was a beautiful place, and Lazarus wished he was lying in a boat on the grey water, resting as the shadows of the hills around it slipped and danced across it to the sound of the wind.

On one shore some small wooden cabins clustered around what he could just make out to be an ancient, ruined church, as a distant bell started to ring out across the valley. Slipping out from the shore, just below the church, was a wooden pier. It looked wide and strong and it stretched out far and deep into the lake, like a thin finger trying to pull at its surface, dragging itself across to reach the centre. Some way out into the lake, the pier seemed to move and bob with the waves and Lazarus realised that from that point onwards, it was a floating pontoon. Resting at its very end was a wide platform and it, like the rest of the pier, was shrouded in high cloth banners, blocking from view anyone who went to walk down it. Lazarus saw movement from the cabins, people leaving them, following the sound of the bell to the church, them all wearing deep-brown cowls, like monks. The church had no roof, but that seemed to add to its charm. It was the perfect place for a religious commune, he thought, remembering what Willie had said. If you wanted to find whatever god you believed in, it was in this kind of place that you'd go looking.

On the other shore was the festival. The traffic was flowing in through a number of gates and people were swarming into the fields, filling them with bright spots of coloured fabric as they pitched their tents. Staring at the ever-increasing crowds, Lazarus wished he could join them, go back to being normal. Instead, he was in a truck with an angel and a dead bloke, and out there in front of them, somewhere at the very bottom of this beautiful and haunting lake, was a doorway to Hell. And who or whatever was on the other side was going to use his dad to smash it to pieces and come flooding through; fallen angels, demons, the Dead . . . It didn't exactly fill him with excitement. Paralysing terror for sure, which he could seriously do without.

Before Lazarus could ask again how they expected to get to the bottom of the lake to find this supposed village, a scream ruptured the moment like the sound of a dog being run over.

A man, his face lined with cracks of wild lunacy, his beard as thick and as orange as rusted wire wool, was standing in front of the Defender, jittering from leg to leg like his feet were on fire and he was trying to put them out. He was naked from the waist up, and wearing a placard strapped to his body. On it Lazarus read the words: 'Danger! Stay Out Of The Lake! Danger!'

'He know something we don't?' he asked as the man continued to scream, slapping his hands against the placard so hard it was making them bleed. Dried splatters of his blood covered the board.

Before Abaddon or Arielle could answer, the man turned his crazed, spittle-fuelled scream into a ferocious and desperate barrage of words, punctuated only with swearing, his eyes wide with the conviction that everything he was saying was of global significance. And with every word he jabbed his fingers either at Lazarus, Arielle and Abaddon, or at the lake. None of it made any sense, particularly the bit about the lake exploding and everyone dying. He even leapt into the air to get across his point that the explosion he was talking about was even more important than everything else he'd said.

Abaddon made to climb out of the Defender, his three-fingered hand reaching for a hidden flintlock.

Arielle rested a hand on his arm, stilling him, her anger now gone.

'No,' she said, like someone calming a guard dog. 'Leave him be.'

'But what he's saying,' said Abaddon, his hand still on the door, 'it is too much of a coincidence . . .'

'Trust me,' said Arielle, allowing a glimmer of a smile to take away her frown, 'he's harmless. And if he's had even the most blurred of visions of what we both know could occur here, it's probably what made him that way in the first place.'

Lazarus latched on to this.

'You mean he's not just a mentalist?'

Arielle looked at Lazarus in the driver's mirror. 'The line between prophet and madman is very thin. Some can take in what they see and process it. Others? It sends them crazy.'

'So how does he know any of it?' Lazarus asked. 'How can we be sure more people don't know what's going on?'

The man stopped yelling, then walked briskly away, his head jutting left and right, like he was expecting someone to jump out on him. He disappeared through the flapping door of a tattered canvas awning, which was tied to a rusting, old mobile home. The whole thing looked like it had been snatched from a trailer park in the US, the kind of place you'd find a shotgun-wielding drunk wearing a string vest, and sitting in the blood of his recently slaughtered family, as he pushed his chubby, sweaty hands into a giant crinkly packet of potato chips and waited for the cops to arrive.

It wasn't exactly inviting.

Arielle gave no answer. And Lazarus had had enough of being kept in the dark. He was sick and tired of not knowing what was round the next corner, of always having to react to what was coming at him to take his head off, instead of being ready for it. If what Abaddon had said about the Black Shard was true, then he wasn't in the mood for sitting around. He wanted this to end. He wanted his dad back, Craig, Clair . . .

Lazarus was out of the back of the Defender before Arielle had a chance to respond.

10
THE MAN WHO SHRIEKED

'Lazarus! We don't have time for this!'

'You get that crazy dead idiot ready to find the village.' Lazarus shouted back. 'I'm going to see what else I can find out.'

He slammed the door and continued on despite yells from Arielle, his eyes on where the mad beard had disappeared through the door of the awning attached to the knackered mobile home.

Inside, the floor was a mess of worn rugs on top of a tatty ground sheet. Two tired folding chairs leaned against the side of the mobile home. From the awning poles hung mobiles like in a children's bedroom. Most were made of twigs and leaves, but one stood out. It was the largest and from the strings on its numerous arms were photos of a girl, each picture showing her at a different age, as if it was a moving monument to her life, dancing and spinning in the faint breaths of wind trapped inside the awning. But other things in the awning spoke of more going on than just the ramblings of a bearded crazy.

In the centre of the awning stood an old dining table held together by brown packing tape. At one side was a stack of diving equipment with a number of wetsuits hanging from one of the awning poles. Under the table were boxes of papers and books. On top of the table was a laptop computer connected to two computer screens, and a collection of other equipment.

'You were listening then?'

The voice was calmer, but still held that same maniacal timbre, like at any moment it would snap and squeal.

The man was standing in the door of the mobile home fully dressed, but the addition of a grubby shirt did little to change his appearance. Insanity didn't just disappear if you pulled some clothes on; it was in his eyes.

'Diver?'

The man nodded.

'Much to see out there?' Lazarus asked, trying to make conversation until he could work out a way to find out what this bloke knew about the lake. There had to be a reason for him pitching what looked like his whole life on to the shore. And if Lazarus was going to be walking into a village in Hell, then he was going to take anything that could give him an edge.

'It's a beautiful place,' said the man, sitting at the table.

Lazarus noticed the crazed look fade a little, like a flame doused by water. 'Been here long?'

The man glanced at the mobile of the girl.

'My daughter,' he said, clearly proud of her. 'Left home three years ago. Chucked in university to come here.'

Lazarus kept quiet, hoping something would soon make sense.

'Rationality,' the man said. 'Always taught her that. But she's thrown it all away. And for what?'

'I'm sorry to intrude,' said Lazarus, having second thoughts after hearing the venom in the man's voice. 'Perhaps I should go . . .'

The man ignored him. 'She's in that commune on the side of the lake. I came to get her back, but she refused to leave. So did I. Three years I've been here. I won't give up either. No father would. Not now. Not after what I've discovered . . .'

Lazarus glanced at all the computer kit. 'You work from here?'

'No one would employ me to do this!' the man laughed. 'What's your name?'

'Lazarus.'

'Biblical.'

'A lot of names are.'

'You're not wrong. I'm Matthew. Pleased to meet you.'

Lazarus was having trouble matching the calm person in front of him with what he'd seen earlier.

'What's all this stuff for?'

'I was, sorry – am – a geologist,' Matthew said, correcting himself. 'Lucrative work too, if you can get it. Oil firms, that kind of thing. Not since I came here though.'

'Three years is a long time to wait for your daughter.'

'I got some work initially, but that dried up, in some cases literally. Then my wife left me . . .'

'So what was all that stuff you were saying about the lake exploding?'

The wildness fired once more in Matthew's eyes. It

was unnerving how it could switch on and off without warning. And he seemed to be turning his attention from the computer to the mobile home, like there was something in it he'd forgotten.

'I have to get people's attention somehow!' Matthew's voice was riddled with alarm. 'Warn them of the danger! But no one will look at my research! They think I'm crazy!'

Lazarus backed away as Matthew grew angry.

'What's this got to do with your daughter?'

Lazarus saw Matthew almost physically work to get himself back under control, his lips moving like he was talking to himself. He tapped a finger against a computer screen.

'She led me here, Lazarus! To this!'

On the screen was a photograph of a lake, the muddy water a deep chocolatey brown. Surrounded by lush green hills, it looked more like a water-filled crater than a river-fed lake.

'Nineteen eighty-six,' Matthew explained, his voice laced with the lucid intensity only a passionate scientist could ever give such a subject, 'this lake killed people!'

'What? How?'

'This is Lake Nyos, West Africa. It sits in a volcano crater dormant for centuries.'

'Dead?'

Matthew shook his head. 'Magma from that volcano, deep below the lake, had been slowly releasing carbon dioxide. But because of the pressure of the water, the CO_2 didn't escape. It just stayed at the bottom, dissolved in the water!'

'Oh, right,' said Lazarus, confused.

'There were other factors, like the lake being blocked from the wind, but the fact remains: this was a bomb waiting to go off!'

Matthew was animated now, arms flailing like an unattended hosepipe on full.

'It had huge amounts of CO_2 sitting in its bowels desperate to escape! And it had to! It had no choice!'

'The volcano erupted?'

'Not exactly,' Matthew answered. 'All it took was a tiny, undetectable seismic flutter, then . . .'

Matthew used his hands to mime the gas rising.

'What happened?'

Matthew was on his feet, hands bursting into the air overhead.

'Boom! The gas burst out with force enough to rip vegetation from the lake's shores! Then it rolled down the mountain, through villages. People were killed in their sleep. Seventeen hundred to be exact, as well as cattle, animals, anything that got in its way. Whole families wiped out! Whole villages. Generations gone in as much time as it takes to make a cup of tea!'

Such an event was difficult to imagine, but the thought of it alone was harrowing.

'Something like that happens, there's nothing you can do. No escape. Too quick, too unexpected.'

Lazarus stared again at the photograph of the lake as Matthew continued to explain that it had happened before in other places on a much smaller scale; hell, even frogs had been found suffocated by CO_2 in low-lying mud puddles . . .

'What's this got to do with Semmerwater?'

Matthew sunk back into his chair and with a calm voice said, 'I think it's going to happen here!'

The words didn't sink in immediately. When they did,

Lazarus didn't know what to do with them.

'Look, I should be getting back.'

Matthew reached out and grabbed his arm, the wildness breaking free.

'Carbon dioxide is building in this lake, Lazarus! I don't know why and I can't explain it.'

Matthew pinned the lake to the horizon with the end of his finger. 'That lake is deeper than it should be, Lazarus!'

'So?'

'I brought my diving equipment to keep myself occupied.'

Matthew stared at Lazarus.

'What do you know of the legend of the lake?'

'The village?'

Matthew smiled. 'That's what I went looking for, the lost village of Simmerdale.'

'Simmerdale?'

'It was called that, but the name changed over time to Semmer. Didn't know what I was expecting to find. It's just a story after all, isn't it?'

Lazarus knew it was anything but, and that if he

spoke of it, he'd make crazy old Matt sound normal.

'Find anything?'

'I knew how deep the lake was,' said Matthew. 'Checked my diving gauge as I went down.'

'Diving alone's insane . . .'

Matthew ignored Lazarus.

'I got to what was supposed to be the maximum depth of the lake, but it wasn't there! The bottom had vanished! It was like getting to the bottom of the stairs in your own house, fully expecting to walk into the hallway, and stepping out into space!'

'Impossible . . .'

'I thought my gauge was reading wrong, but it was fine. I kept diving, went right to the limit I'm qualified to dive to, still no lake bed! I tried again, but the same result each time! I found something else too—'

Lazarus cut in with, 'What are you saying?'

'I don't know,' sighed Matthew. 'I can't explain it. No one will believe me.'

Lazarus wasn't entirely surprised; the hermit lifestyle didn't exactly help his cause.

'I even built a remote-control submersible.'

'Did it get to the bottom?'

Matthew didn't answer the question, just looked again at the mobile home. What the hell was in there that was bugging him so much?

'It just kept on diving and diving until everything went dead, like it had been physically snatched from the water. I've never been able to recover it, not even a bit of wreckage. All I've got is the footage of what it saw, and the CO_2 readings, which are off the chart.'

Lazarus changed the subject.

'Your daughter?'

Matthew picked up a pair of huge binoculars from off the floor.

'This is the closest I get to her,' he said. 'But I'm not giving up. I have to get her back; if the lake explodes and she's still here . . .'

Matthew's voice hit fade-out and Lazarus noticed how he seemed suddenly smaller, like the weight of his daughter being so estranged was crushing him. As Matthew slipped into his thoughts, Lazarus took the chance and was out through the flapping door quick and silent.

Walking back to the Defender, he glanced out over

the lake. The grey water was as glass, though it had more of a shimmering quality to it, like a heat wave blurring the horizon. It looked nothing like the African lake Matthew had shown him. This was a place of quiet and solitude, not somewhere a giant gas fart was lying in wait under a lake, poised to wipe out the masses.

Lazarus climbed into the rear of the Defender.

'Back then,' said Arielle.

'Observant.'

'Learn anything?'

Lazarus explained what had got Matthew so excited. 'It's only stuff that would be of use if I was studying a geology degree,' he said dismissively. 'Something's bothering him, but I don't know if it's because he's mad or scared. He thinks the lake is deeper than it should be and that it might explode.'

Lazarus sat down and closed his eyes, weary from Matthew's intensity.

'Hungry?'

Arielle handed him a can about the size of a family tin of soup from her never-ending supply of self-heating meals.

'You mean you're not going to treat me to a slap-up feast in a restaurant?'

Arielle smiled and shook her head.

'Guessed as much,' said Lazarus. 'What about the village? Have you worked out how Abaddon will get there to bring back the other half of the Black Shard?'

He dug a spoon into the tin, hoped that whatever he was about to eat tasted better than the last one he'd had. 'I've found some diving equipment. Useless to Abaddon, but at least he'll look the part.'

The creak of Abaddon's skin interrupted the conversation.

'I will go to the village and retrieve the other half of the Black Shard. You have my word.'

'Great,' said Lazarus, the spoon hovering before his mouth. 'The word of a dead bloke. What could possibly go wrong?'

11
TWISTED WRONGED PARADISE

'What's he doing?'

It was late afternoon. Lazarus, food sitting heavy in his stomach, was standing at the lake's edge with Arielle. Abaddon was a few steps in front, his booted feet lapped by the gently moving water. Hanging from a rope draped over the dead priest's shoulders were two canvas bags from the back of Arielle's Defender. Each was filled with rocks they had spent the past ten minutes collecting from the shore of Lake Semmerwater.

The day was turning grey, like it just wanted everyone to feel a little bit morose and damp. This was supposed to be summer, thought Lazarus. What had happened to the sun?

'Something he's been avoiding doing for a very long time,' Arielle said. 'Finishing what he started.'

'And the rocks? Some kind of penance?'

Arielle shook her head. 'Think, Lazarus; if Abaddon walks into that lake, what's going to stop him from floating back up to the surface?'

'What do you mean, walk into the lake?'

Abaddon was standing utterly still, like his body had finally accepted its fate and become truly petrified in death.

Arielle nodded at the mobile home. 'Despite what you may think about all the crazy things Matthew said about the lake, it got Abaddon's attention.'

'The giant exploding gas bubble stuff? Seriously?'

'No,' said Arielle. 'What he said about the lake bed sinking, getting deeper.'

'Why?'

Abaddon stepped forward, then stood still again, like he was preparing himself, meditating almost.

'Remember what Abaddon said, about him once paying a house call? He's done this before, Lazarus. He came back here, a long time ago now, before I locked him in that cave. He walked out into the centre of the lake to see what he had done. He found his village at the bottom of it, or some foul shadow of it at least. I do not know exactly what he found. He has never spoken of it.'

'Simmerdale?'

Arielle nodded, her eyebrows raised.

'I only know it was called that because Matthew mentioned it.'

'I tried to get him to talk,' said Arielle, 'but he said nothing, gave nothing, just said to me that to tell or speak of it was to risk too much.'

'Is everything he says always laden with such doom and gloom?'

'Comes with the territory,' said Arielle. 'Being Abaddon seems to be the very essence of doom and gloom.'

Abaddon removed his hat to reveal his deep-brown leathery scalp. It looked like the crust on a chocolate pudding that had been left in a baker's shop window for a month or two. He then held out his hat to Lazarus in his three-fingered hand.

Lazarus took it.

'My weapons?'

'Safely stowed in the truck,' said Arielle. 'Sure you don't need any more?'

The only answer she got was Abaddon pulling two vicious-looking single-hand scythes from a belt hidden from view. Then he was moving. He didn't turn, didn't speak, just started to walk into the water, slowly and deliberately, each footfall sinking with awful purpose beneath the waves.

Into the lake he slipped, edging deeper and deeper. He didn't put a step wrong, just seemed to glide out and away from them like he was standing on an invisible escalator. It was eerie as hell, like watching someone slip helpless into Hades.

After a couple of minutes, all that remained visible was Abaddon's shoulders and head. Then the water was lapping at his chin. For a few brief moments, the top of his head could still be seen, like a smooth lump of wood floating on the lake's surface. At last, silently, the water swallowed him and he was gone. And there were no bubbles to trace; Abaddon, Lazarus knew, didn't breathe.

Despite Abaddon having now completely disappeared, Lazarus kept staring out over the water, half expecting to see him bob up in a spray of water, gasping for air.

'Did that really just happen?' he asked, but before

Arielle could answer, and for the first time since the incident with the motorbike, he sensed death.

Arielle snapped round like a spinning top.

'Lazarus?'

Lazarus couldn't breathe, had his eyes squeezed shut, was doubled over. His stomach was churning and he could taste acid in his mouth.

Pushing the nausea deep down, Lazarus pulled his eyes open. The Dead were close. But where were they?

Arielle spoke again, her voice harsh and urgent. 'Where, Lazarus? I see no one! Speak to me!'

With a final squeeze of his eyes, Lazarus took a deep breath, recovered, but still kept himself bent over; if he stood up too quickly, he'd pass out.

'Close,' he said, then almost on cue heard the revving of an engine.

A Range Rover swung into the parking area in front of the lake, its windows greyed out. Two figures dressed in brown cowls stepped out from the rear doors of the vehicle as the driver's window slid into the door. As they made their way towards Matthew's camper van, the driver showed his face. It was pale, with eyes hidden behind sunglasses. For a moment, he just stared, then with a polite nod, he disappeared once more as the window oozed up from the door, and sped from the parking area in a spray of gravel. Lazarus turned his attention to the two figures now almost at Matthew's temporary home. One was basketball-player tall, the other the size of a child.

Arielle walked over to him, one hand inside her jacket on the hilt of her sword. The other she rested on his back as he slowly stood up.

'What are they after?' asked Arielle, sword still in its scabbard, but her hand restless. 'I thought they had come for us!'

'Matthew said his daughter is part of that commune Willie mentioned,' said Lazarus pointing. 'That place over there with the ruined church and cabins.'

Arielle looked to see the Range Rover pulling into the commune and disappear behind a cabin.

The two figures were now at the camper van, the door of the awning flapping in the wind like road-kill wings.

'Are they occupied?' Arielle asked. 'Do they have the Dead in them?'

Lazarus didn't answer. The tall figure entered through

the awning attached to Matthew's mobile home. The one Lazarus assumed must be a child simply waited outside.

'Did you get anything from the driver?'

Lazarus nodded and said, 'But something isn't right.' He picked up a stone from the beach and lobbed it hard across the lake. It managed seven skips before it was swallowed, but each bounce seemed to play out in slow motion. It reminded him of how he'd felt after the crash, when he'd been left paralysed on the ground to be eaten to death. Abaddon had referred to the figure that had ripped him from the Defender and tried to kill him, as one of the Fallen, an angel trapped in Hell. Not so trapped any more, thought Lazarus.

The ripples from the stone faded and Lazarus stole a look back towards the mobile home. The tall figure was now standing outside too. Though he could not see beyond the shadow cast by the hoods, he knew they were staring at him. For a moment they held each other's gaze. Then the tall figure turned and slipped back in through the awning's door, stooping low. The smaller figure turned to follow, but first it removed its hood.

Lazarus's heart didn't just skip a beat, it stopped dead

with a crashing thud. It was a little girl, no older than seven or eight. But what struck him most was that she reminded him of someone . . . *Abaddon!*

'That tall one,' said Arielle. 'It recognised you.'

Lazarus's gut felt like someone had just filled it with liquid concrete. 'The girl,' he tried, but was unable to get the words out, and they stuck in his throat like badly chewed meat.

'It was one of the Fallen,' said Arielle. 'And I'd put money on it being the same one we met on the moors last night.'

'But the girl, Arielle; didn't you notice it?'

'What?'

'She looked like Abaddon!' The words spat out of him like poison. 'And I know that sounds insane. But it's true!'

Arielle choked on Lazarus's words. 'But Abaddon's daughter's dead! She has to be! Even if one of the Dead did take her, there's no way she could still be alive. Not now!'

'I know that,' said Lazarus. 'But it's a bit of a coincidence, isn't it?'

Arielle was silent.

'What if that was her?' Lazarus, picked up another stone as something else bubbled to the surface of his mind. 'And another thing – why have the Dead left Matthew alone all this time? And who was the driver? Why did he stare at us?'

Arielle joined Lazarus and threw a stone herself. It bounced right across the lake to disappear into the reeds on the distant shore.

'Show off.'

Arielle found another stone. 'What do you mean about Matthew?'

'He's been here since his daughter joined the commune, right? And in all that time, the Dead have let him just do what he's been doing, talking strange and drawing attention to the lake. But if what you and Abaddon have said about this place is true, why would the Dead want someone drawing any attention to it at all? Why not just get rid of him?'

Lazarus threw another stone. 'It's a trap.'

'Sometimes,' said Arielle, 'a distraction is the best way of making sure something isn't noticed.'

'Don't talk crap.'

'Think about it,' said Arielle. 'Matthew's been saying all that stuff about the lake for years and no one's taken any notice. They've been ignoring him. The louder he shouts, the more deaf people become! Ask any prophet; they'll tell you that's how it works.'

'Seems a backwards way of doing things.'

'Effective though,' said Arielle.

'So what are they up to? If it really was that fallen angel from the moor, why aren't we fighting for our lives? I don't like it!'

'Neither do I, Lazarus.' Arielle's voice betrayed stress. 'I now wonder if it is because they are not afraid. Of you, me, Abaddon, why we're here, anything!'

'Should they be?'

'The Fallen, Lazarus, have never made it through the veil to escape Hell. It's one thing for the Dead to get through, but them? The consequences are too awful to imagine.'

'Not good then.'

Arielle shook her head. 'But no prison is truly secure, Lazarus. Not even Hell. Things can slip out. The faint whispers the Fallen mutter seeping through the cracks between the voids of the deepest darknesses, but not them, Lazarus . . . Not *them*!'

'You actually sound scared. And it's not exactly encouraging.'

'This is no time to be flippant,' Arielle suddenly snapped back, her hair whipping round like the snakes of Medusa. 'The Fallen have escaped, Lazarus! Hell has failed!'

To see her like this terrified Lazarus. Yes, she was a little unhinged, and yes she drank too much, but there was a presence about her that gave him courage. Now though, without warning, he'd seen a chink in her armour. And the thought that there were things out there she couldn't protect him from vaporised his confidence with the power of an A-bomb.

Arielle hadn't finished. 'This could be the end, Lazarus, do you not understand that? This is not some teenage prank you can scrape your knees on and laugh about over a stolen bottle of beer!'

'I . . . I never said it was,' Lazarus spluttered, trying to regain some composure.

'Well, perhaps you should just grow up! Either you

start taking this seriously or we have already lost!'

Arielle's attack turned Lazarus's fear to raw anger. 'Got anything else to say, or are you just going to leave it at that?'

Arielle stared hard, breathed deep, then calmly started to explain. 'A war split the angels, Lazarus. Humanity was its cause.'

'How?'

A distant look slipped across Arielle's eyes, like she wasn't just staring into the distance, but through time itself.

'We angels were born knowing the beginning and the end of all things. But you? You had a unique perspective to grow from nothing, to learn, to discover!'

'How did that cause a war?'

'You do not understand how precious a gift your life is, Lazarus. We thought we were so perfect, so pure. But seeing what you had? Something that in its mess, its brokenness, made even our own beauty pale? Can you imagine what that was like? A jealous angel is an awesome thing, Lazarus. And terrible.'

Lazarus heard a shudder in Arielle's voice. He didn't

like to imagine what a fight would be like between Arielle and one of her own, never mind a war.

'What happened?'

'A faction wanted humanity erased. They believed you to be an abomination; imperfect beings but with the capacity to experience life so perfectly. They were unable to accept that any creation but themselves could have such a thing. It began as nothing more than rumbling, heated arguments, but then the words ended and the fighting began.'

There was a moment of silence as Arielle, visibly shaken by what she was recalling, closed her eyes. When she opened them again, her voice held a calmness both awful and terrifying.

'The war was ferocious, with no quarter given by either side. The very heavens were splattered with the blood of the dead and the dying, their spirits scattered to the winds that chase stars. But in the end, humanity was saved, though it was a close call. Those who could not accept your existence lost the war and were given a chance to repent. Those who did were given a second chance. Those who did not were locked away from everything for eternity. It was an awful punishment, but the only one which could be given. They are the Fallen, Lazarus. And they are terrible!'

Lazarus couldn't stop the question that slipped from his mouth. 'So which side were you on?'

'Both,' said Arielle unexpectedly. 'Double-agent. Sent behind lines to collect information. Befriend the enemy. One in particular . . .'

Lazarus saw Arielle wipe away tears before they fell.

'You're not telling me everything, are you?'

'I am telling you what you need to know,' Arielle snapped, but caught herself and softened her voice a little. 'Hell is home to the Fallen. And as added torment, they are sent the worst of humanity, those whose souls are so black and rotten that all hope is lost. It is a twisted, wronged paradise, Lazarus! Eden ripped apart and bleeding . . . You have no idea . . .'

Lazarus left Arielle with her thoughts and walked back to the Defender, opening the passenger door to reach over to the centre seat. When he turned back towards Arielle, in his hand was the spike, that angelic weapon that had somehow become a part of him. The thorns on the handle had slipped through his palm and were now jabbing out the back of his hand, long, sharp and deadly. He felt the warmth of his own blood splash across his skin, but didn't feel any pain. Just having the weapon clenched in his fist sent such a wave of power through him that he had to steady himself against the wing of the truck.

For the next few moments, everything that had happened since all this had begun washed over him, threatening to drown him, almost as though the spike was acting as a hard drive to his soul. And with each memory came something else, something deeper. He couldn't explain it, but he suddenly felt utterly connected to everything he'd done, like every tiny moment of every experience could be drawn on to help him with what he had to do next.

Lazarus pushed himself away from the Defender and walked towards Arielle.

'You said they're no longer afraid, right?'

Arielle nodded.

Lazarus raised his spike and pointed it at Matthew's mobile home. 'How's about we go change that?'

12
SPLINTERED REMAINS

The explosion blasted Lazarus off his feet before he'd taken a single step. Metal and glass shards sliced into him as he sailed through the air to land hard on his back on the stony shore. The blast killed all sound and Lazarus thought his eardrums were about to be sucked out of his skull. Pain clawed his nerves, sending a barrage of agony shrieking into his head to try and burst his eyes, as pebbles stabbed into him. He caught sight of Arielle flying further and landing just as heavily, though she was immediately up on her feet, her lank hair and long coat shivering and fluttering like the feathers of a bird killed in the shock wave.

For a moment the air was rich with the sweet, choking smell of fire and fuel. A ghostly shroud of smoke rolled across the shore as the shattered remnants of what had once been Matthew's mobile home rained down. And Matthew too, no doubt, thought Lazarus grimly.

Blinking dust from his eyes he rolled over and pushed himself up on to his elbows, then used the spike in his hand to gain some purchase in the ground and heave himself to his feet. He ached like hell, as though he'd just gone ten rounds with a pro boxer.

'Lazarus!'

Lazarus kept his eyes on what was left of the mobile home as Arielle strode over, sweeping the hair out of her face. It was flecked with blood and her hair was ghosted white with dust. A sliver of metal was sticking out of her left arm.

Lazarus nodded at the wound. 'You want me to . . . ?'

Arielle reached up, yanked the metal out, didn't flinch.

'I'll take that as a no.'

The blast had split Matthew's mobile home in two. It looked like a great and mighty axe had been brought down on it in an act of unrepentant brutality. The roof had been ripped back like the lid of a tuna can. Some of the poles were still standing, but the ragged remains of the awning itself clung to them like washing left on the line.

Lazarus stepped forward as a strong hand rested on his shoulder to halt him.

'I go first,' said Arielle. 'My job, remember?'

Lazarus was given no chance to respond or argue; Arielle moved with such swift grace that he had to break into a jog to just keep up.

They reached the outer circle of the debris from the explosion. The ground was scorched, but above, a grey cloud was already weeping, and the faint rain was beginning to clean the ground.

'Touch nothing,' said Arielle, now making her way carefully between the smashed flames and spirals of smoke that covered the ground ahead. 'If you see something, tell me first, yes?'

Lazarus didn't respond, simply started to make his own way through the wreckage. He had no idea what he was looking for – *anything* – that could give some clue as to why this had just happened. It hadn't escaped his attention that he saw no body parts, no blood.

He made to step left, stumbled, tried to catch his balance, was too late. The ground came up fast, but he managed to break his fall with his hands.

'Watch yourself,' said Arielle, not even turning to see if he was OK.

Lazarus pushed himself back up then spotted something fluttering in the breeze to his right. It was a photograph, scorched a little, but still intact. He reached for it, ignoring what Arielle had said about telling her first before touching anything. He stood up. The image staring back was Matthew's daughter. Lazarus folded the photograph and stowed it in his pocket.

A shout came from Arielle, and Lazarus turned to see that she was holding up a smouldering laptop. He had a feeling that it was too damaged to be of any use, but it was probably worth having a look at anyway.

Lazarus continued towards the mobile home, eyes scanning the ground. He was trying to come up with an explanation for what had happened: the explosion; that it had happened the day they arrived at the lake; the fallen angel; the smell of death on those who had entered the awning; the completely freaky lack of any body parts or blood . . .

Arielle reached the mobile home and took a careful

step up into it. Lazarus wondered why the whole thing wasn't a mass of flames burning white hot and melting what was left, but then this wasn't the movies, this was real: the shock wave had caused the damage and blasted the place into a million scattered pieces like a burst bag of Lego.

Lazarus followed Arielle, who then made her way through the ruins and sat down at the splintered remains of a table. She leaned down to the floor, brushed away debris, and pulled out a half-drunk bottle of whisky.

'What are the odds?' said Lazarus.

Arielle heaved the cork from the bottle with her teeth and took a slug. 'I'm racking my brain for an explanation,' she said, wiping her mouth with her sleeve, 'but I'm coming up blank. You?'

Instead of sitting down, Lazarus started to shuffle through what was left of the cupboards and drawers inside where Matthew had spent the best part of three years of his life. He shook his head as he opened one after another, searching for what, he hadn't the faintest idea.

'And why now, Lazarus? Why leave him be all this time, then do this? What was the point?'

'What about the bodies?'

'Must've escaped at the last minute,' said Arielle. 'If that was one of the Fallen, then they could easily have taken Matthew and destroyed whatever it was he was doing here.'

'Well, at least we now know there was something here that they didn't want us to find,' sighed Lazarus, and shut the cupboard he'd just looked through, moving on to the last remaining drawer. The front of it fell off, spilling the contents across the floor and over his feet like vomit. He knelt down to shuffle through them with his hands. Something sharp sliced his fingers, drew blood.

Arielle fell quiet. Lazarus glanced up at her and saw confusion written into a blank stare. She opened the knackered laptop and Lazarus was surprised to hear the thing boot up.

'You're kidding me,' he said, almost laughing. 'It survived? How?'

'It's a strange thing,' Arielle replied, now punching her thin fingers across the keyboard and navigating her way around Matthew's hard drive, 'but often, in scenes of the most impossible, clearly unsurvivable devastation, you will find the inexplicable; an undamaged bottle of milk on a doorstep after an explosion that's ripped the rest of the street to pieces. An unharmed child running from a building collapsing in flames. A bottle of whisky and a laptop computer covered in the remains of a ruined mobile home. It happens.'

'Anything on it?'

'A folder of movie files. They all seem to be of the lake. You said he was a diver, right?'

Lazarus nodded. 'That's how he found out about the lake being deeper than it should be. He had a submersible, too, but that it disappeared.'

A sharp intake of breath from Arielle hooked Lazarus out of his thoughts.

'What is it?'

Arielle nodded at the screen, tapped it with her fingers. 'See for yourself.'

Lazarus moved round to sit next to her as she hit 'Play'. The sound quality was a bit rubbish, mainly the sound of electric motors, the image a little murky.

'What is it?' Lazarus asked, squinting his eyes in a pointless attempt to make the image clearer.

'I think it's from Matthew's submersible,' said Arielle. 'Must've been taken before it disappeared.'

'But it's just grey. There's nothing to see.'

'Keep watching.'

Something on the screen came into focus. Lazarus wasn't sure what it was, but the water in the image seemed to be swirling towards something hidden in the murk.

Whatever it was, the submersible sounded like it was beginning to struggle against the current. Lazarus continued to stare, trying to come up with something in his mind that looked like what he was now seeing come into focus on the screen; water swirling, dragging mud and weeds into it, spinning them round into a violent vortex that shimmered like sunlight was bouncing off it. Then something did.

'It's a bloody whirlpool!' Lazarus was unable to comprehend that what he was seeing was for real. 'But . . . that's impossible . . .'

'Why?'

'Because you need a current of some sort to have one,' Lazarus replied. 'And this place, Lake Semmerwater? It's not exactly thrashing about is it?'

'What else?'

Lazarus thought for a second, then the impossible nature of what was on the screen hit him like a prize-fighter's right hook. 'It's under the surface . . . but I can see the top of it! That can't be right . . . I've never seen anything like this . . . an underwater whirlpool?'

Something darted across the screen and into the mouth of the whirlpool. Lazarus nearly fell off his seat. 'Did you just see that? A fish just got sucked into it! How strong is that thing?'

The film shuddered and stopped.

Arielle and Lazarus were silent. Lazarus spoke for them both.

'Abaddon . . . he's walking right into that, isn't he?'

13
OMENS

'We have to stop him!'

It was the first time Lazarus had heard Arielle sound like she didn't know what to do next. It was unnerving and the exact opposite of what he needed. Not that he really knew what that was exactly, but something to hold on to and give him a sense of hope would be useful. Something that would give him a little bit of a hold on reality while all around him the world was dissolving to chaos.

'We can't,' Lazarus replied. 'You know that! Get a grip!'

He was doing everything he could to remain calm. It wasn't easy. What he really wanted to do was scream out loud till his lungs burst, grab Arielle and drag something useful out of her. They had to work out what to do next; it had become very clear to him that whatever plan Arielle had actually had for any of this had been loose to say the least. And 'Stop Hell' didn't quite seem enough.

'Abaddon's in the lake, Arielle. We can't follow him; it's impossible.'

Arielle leaped out of the mobile home, right over Lazarus's head. She pulled Matthew's diving equipment from the scorched wreckage lying about outside on the shore. It looked amazingly unscathed. But that still wasn't enough to convince Lazarus to use it.

'It's totally screwed!' he shouted, even though he hadn't a clue if the stuff was working or not. He just wanted to shut down Arielle's idea before it had a chance to take its first breath and they were both heading off for a swim. 'And even if it is undamaged, there's no way I'm going to put my life on the line, diving with no experience. I can't even swim, remember?'

'It looks fine,' said Arielle, giving the equipment a shake, as if that would in some way prove her point. 'It's the only option we have! We need Abaddon! We can't risk losing him, or the Black Shard! You don't understand!'

Lazarus opened his mouth to reply, even thought of a few words, but as soon as they started to form in his mouth they became no more than dust blown away on his breath.

He stared out at the lake. It looked peaceful, serene. Not the kind of place you'd ever expect to have a powerful and impossible whirlpool hidden in its depths, a village lost to legend, and a dead priest . . .

Lazarus spotted an upturned boat on the shore, green paint fading and chipped. At its side was an ageing kayak. It had been painted black, with a white skull and crossbones on it. It was filled with water and looked just a little sad and lonely. So the kayak was out, but the boat – that had possibilities. It didn't look big, but it would get them out on to the water. But floating about on the lake wouldn't help Abaddon. If anything it would only add to the danger they were in. Here, on the shore, they were exposed. But out on a boat? They would be sitting ducks!

Desperate for an idea to present itself, no matter how small, Lazarus again started to search through what was left of Matthew's mobile home. Surely there was a clue here as to what was going on! Yet wherever he looked, he found nothing; just more and more junk that he didn't understand, or had been rendered useless by the explosion. He finally gave up and made to follow Arielle.

It was as he was nearing the door that his left foot crunched through something on the floor, like a hole had opened up. Lazarus looked down. His foot had sunk into the scrappy, grubby carpet.

'Lazarus? What is it?'

Lazarus didn't answer, dropped to the floor and peeled back the carpet.

'There's something here!' he yelled out. 'A hidden compartment under the floor!'

Arielle was with him in a breath.

The carpet pulled back, Lazarus could see that his foot had gone through a section of wood covering up a hole in the floor. He must've just missed it on the way in. And it probably only gave way because it had been damaged by the explosion.

Lazarus pulled at the section of wood. It came away in evil-looking splinters to reveal a small, hidden compartment. Reaching in, he lifted out a CD and some papers. In the papers he found some of Matthew's notes. They mentioned the whirlpool, the mystery of the lake's unknown depth. They also contained a map of the lake.

'Look at this,' said Lazarus, holding out the map to show Arielle. He pointed at a red blot on the map. 'The location of the whirlpool, see? He labelled it WP: whirlpool, right? It has to be! And look . . .'

Lazarus pointed at the date on the map; it was only a few days ago.

'I'm guessing that this is the reason for the explosion and Matthew's disappearance. When he discovered this, something had to be done.'

Lazarus remembered how when he'd spoken to Matthew, he'd kept glancing back at the mobile home. He guessed now that in his hands was the reason why.

Arielle dropped a finger to something Matthew had drawn on the map stretching from the shore into the lake. It came to an end at the red blot.

'And this?'

Lazarus looked at the map, then up and across the lake. He pointed to where the lake lapped the shore below the old ruined church. 'It's the pier. The end of it floats, you can see it bobbing on the water.'

'According to Matthew's map, it leads from that commune to directly above the whirlpool. And I don't believe in coincidences.'

Lazarus realised what the whirlpool was.

'It's the veil, isn't it? Or a permanent weakness in it, like Abaddon said.'

Arielle's face was as stone.

Lazarus kept talking. 'And at the bottom of it lies Abaddon's village. And Hell.'

Arielle held up the CD. 'So what's on this, then?' She quickly retrieved the damaged laptop, slipped the CD into the drive and started to click through the files. The images, like the one of the whirlpool, were all blurry to begin with. The first three films, clearly done by a handheld camera, were all of the ruined church. They watched a procession walk from it down and across the pier, and out to the platform. Lazarus couldn't work out what was going on, but then, on the third film, saw a splash in the water.

'They've thrown something off the pier!' he gasped.

'Something,' muttered Arielle, 'or someone . . .'

Lazarus was shocked. 'Why would they throw a person off the pier?'

Arielle was quiet.

A further two files showed the same again, each one ending with a splash of water at the end of the platform. On neither were they able to work out what it was that was cast into the water, only that it happened, and that it made a pretty big splash.

The last file was clearly filmed much closer. Lazarus wondered if Matthew had been searching for his daughter when he'd taken it, because although it was of another procession, it was obvious that he'd been focusing on faces, or at least trying to. It was impossible to see most of them, hidden as they were in the shadows behind the cowls they all wore. In the last few moments, before the film came to an end, the image zoomed in on a figure Lazarus recognised immediately. And the camera stayed on it for an unnerving length of time.

It was the figure from the moors, the figure who'd entered Matthew's mobile home moments before it exploded. And when it turned to the camera, let its cowl slip backwards, and wagged its finger at it, as though it was chastising a naughty child, Lazarus went cold. Once Matthew had filmed this, he thought, his days had been numbered.

'He must've filmed this only a couple of days ago,' said Arielle. 'It all ties in with what he found out about the whirlpool.'

Lazarus agreed. 'He made a connection between what they were doing and the whirlpool, tried to get closer to find out more, and was spotted. But it doesn't explain why they've not come after us since that motorbike forced us off the road.'

Arielle closed the laptop. 'They think they've got a measure of us now, Lazarus, and probably view us as a mild irritation, maybe even something of amusement. The arrogance of the Fallen is one of their failings. And possibly our only advantage.'

'In other words,' said Lazarus, 'no matter what we throw at them, they think they can handle it?'

'More than handle it,' Arielle replied. 'They're probably itching to see what we're going to do next so that they can watch it fail then crush us like ants.'

Lazarus shook his head. 'If it's all the same

with you, I'll ignore that.'

Arielle picked up the papers, the map and the laptop, and stood up, stepping out of the mobile home and making her way towards the Defender. She looked smaller, like she was carrying something so heavy, her shoulders and back were having difficulty dealing with it.

When Lazarus caught up, he pointed to the ruined church. 'We have to go up there. We need to find out what the Dead are planning, why the Fallen are involved, and what exactly they're throwing off the pier into the whirlpool.'

Arielle kept walking.

'I'm talking to you!'

Arielle stopped.

Lazarus jogged forwards and stood between her and the Defender. 'If you have a better idea, then how's about you let me in on it?'

Arielle wasn't listening.

'What is it?'

Arielle was staring out across the Lake. Lazarus did the same.

It was getting late now, and the sky was letting the

horizon pull darkness to it like a blanket across a bed. And it was strangely silent, realised Lazarus. He wasn't one for thinking about stuff like omens, but whether he believed in them or not, the very clear lack of any birdcalls fluttering through the air was more than a little unnerving.

'There!'

Whatever Arielle had seen, Lazarus couldn't make it out. He squeezed his eyes to get a better focus and it became clear . . . Then something broke the surface of the lake, and started to make its slow way towards them.

His jaw dropped open.

'Abaddon . . .'

14

HELL'S HALFWAY HOUSE

Arielle sprinted into the lake, kicking up a spray of grey water into the evening light. Forcing his legs into a run, Lazarus joined her, and the cold of the water seeped through his boots and trousers to sting his skin.

Abaddon was still some way out, and all they could see of him was his shoulders. The water slipped from him, almost like it was trying to get out of his way. He moved with a relentlessness that spoke more of the kind of momentum a truck would have if its brakes failed on a hill, than normal human motion. Abaddon, it seemed, had a weight to him that went beyond just the walking corpse he occupied, and Lazarus could almost feel it. And he knew that the source of that otherworldly weight lay with the Black Shard he carried in his chest.

Arielle was waist deep now, but Lazarus, wading hard,

was gaining on her. When he finally managed to catch up he could see that Abaddon was walking awkwardly. And it wasn't just because he was dead, or because he was coming out of the lake with the waves breaking against him. It was because he was carrying something heavy.

A faint gust of nausea washed over Lazarus. He instinctively pushed it back and quickly chalked it down as a natural response to the fact that he was standing in a freezing lake trying to rescue a walking corpse; it was enough to make anyone feel a little queasy.

Movement caught his eye and Lazarus whipped round, found himself gazing across at the pier. Behind the cloth banners that lined it he saw the flickering images of people on the platform at its end and realised that what had caught his attention was something being thrown into the water. Another weirdo going through the motions, he thought and quickly got back to what was happening now.

'What is it?' Lazarus asked, his teeth chattering now with the cold. 'What the hell's he gone and brought back with him?'

Arielle didn't answer, just kept on wading.

Lazarus did the same, wasn't sure he wanted to find out, but now he could look at nothing else. His eyes were fixed on whatever Abaddon was holding, like an invisible thread was holding them and forcing them to look. Close to pulling his eyes right out.

Then, in a singular moment where Lazarus felt like he'd suddenly been sucked into a black hole, his limbs pulled from his body by the very force of it, the thing in Abaddon's arms broke the surface.

'Shit . . . it's Craig . . .'

Again, nausea came at Lazarus, and again he punched it back down. No way was he going to let mere queasiness get in the way now, not with the sudden appearance of the only real mate he'd ever been able to count on, and someone he thought he'd never see again.

'Whatever you do, don't mention the girl, OK?' said Arielle. 'What we saw, we can't be totally sure of. But if Abaddon gets wind of it, he'll lose focus. Now is not the time, believe me!'

'But what if it was his daughter? Shouldn't we tell him?'

'Do as I say, Lazarus!' hissed Arielle. 'We must keep

control of Abaddon! Understand?'

Lazarus nodded and turned his focus back on Craig. Of all the things he'd expected to see, his best mate wasn't it. How could he be? Hadn't the Dark taken him? Where the hell had Abaddon found him?

More nausea, this time stronger . . .

But it wasn't impossible, and when Lazarus drew closer, doing his best to ignore the swimming sensation threatening to engulf his brain, when he could actually see the pale, lifeless colour of Craig's skin, and the way his soaking-wet red hair stuck to it, he gave up trying to force back the tears. Craig was bruised and badly cut. Wherever he'd been, it looked like something had worked on him good and proper at trying to smash him to pieces.

'Abaddon . . .' said Arielle as they at last met him, obviously trying to say so much with just one word. But Abaddon did not stop, simply kept on walking, heading to shore.

'The boy is alive,' Abaddon gurgled as water bubbled out of his mouth.

'The village, Abaddon,' said Arielle, wading after him. 'The Black Shard . . .'

Abaddon stopped and Arielle and Lazarus caught up. He stared at them from behind his blind, eyeless sockets.

'The lake has changed,' he said. 'Where the bottom was, it is no more. It has sunk deeper than you can imagine. The village—'

Abaddon coughed out grey water.

'The village has slipped. The shadow it once was is no longer. The weight of Hell has dragged it down deep.'

'But if it's not where it was at the bottom of the lake, how did you get there? How did you come back?'

'A current swept me there,' Abaddon replied, and Lazarus immediately thought about the whirlpool. 'I was lost to it, unable to fight it. It swept me away and when all movement stopped, I was home. But it is a changed place, Arielle. Worse than before.'

Lazarus was shivering violently now, the cold gnawing at him. And being this deep in water unnerved him. That he could still touch the bottom made no difference. He couldn't swim and had to fight the panic bubbling in his stomach, ignore the voice in his head screaming at him that he was about to drown. Arielle didn't stop her questions.

'And Craig?'

'The village is occupied, angel! Filled with the Dead! It is a halfway house between Hell and here, but for what reason I do not know. I had not the time. The boy I found by fortune and luck, that is all. He was amongst the Dead when they attacked me.'

Lazarus choked. 'Craig attacked you?'

'I did not say that,' replied Abaddon. 'I found him in a house, bound and gagged. The Dead were preparing him for some ritual, I think. I put a stop to it.'

Arielle made to say something, but Abaddon stilled her with a shake of his head.

'The Black Shard, the half I broke off to nail the village to the skin of Hell, was not there. It is gone!'

Lazarus wasn't sure, but he thought he almost heard some betrayal of emotion in Abaddon's voice. Not much, but just enough.

Arielle said nothing.

Abaddon looked down at Craig. 'What they were going to do to him, I do not know. And I did not see the girl. The Black Shard inside me aided me enough to slip from the village with Craig, and back into the current that swept me there in the first place. It works both ways, it seems; allows you to travel in and out.'

Lazarus reached out to touch Craig, as though he needed a physical sign that this was completely for real and he wasn't making it up. His fingers slipped across Craig's forehead. His skin was icy cold and slimy, like touching a fish on ice. Then something blasted out of it and through Lazarus, a wave of such intense and ferocious hatred, that it knocked him off his feet and under the water.

Lazarus thrashed his arms. He couldn't find the bottom of the lake. But that wasn't possible; where they were, it wasn't deep enough . . . His lungs were threatening to explode; he'd been taken off guard, hadn't had time to heave in a decent breath before he went under. His fear of water took over. Terror shot through him like an electric shock. All he could think about was drowning, sinking into the lake, his lungs filled with water.

Panic seized him. Then nausea kicked in again, but this time with such a force that he was sure it would rip him apart from the inside, peel him away in reverse. Lazarus was helpless to stop it hitting him hard, not with the water forcing its way into his mouth, down into his lungs, like thin silvery fingers were trying to prise apart his lips, force his jaw open, and drown him.

He coughed, felt his stomach lurch like something had punched it, and vomit streaked out in front of him to swirl in the water like an oil slick. There was nothing he could do; he had to breathe, and that would be it . . .

Fresh air!

Lazarus gasped as an iron grip ripped him from the clutches of the lake and out into the open. Abaddon held him up high, shook him like a wet puppy, then dumped him back on his feet. Craig was now over Abaddon's shoulder, hanging there like the carcass of a dead pig.

Lazarus sucked oxygen into his lungs, pulled it in with great heaves of his chest, but it wasn't enough. Whatever had flung him off Craig, smashed through him and almost made him drown in his own puke, was still here . . .

15

LIQUID BLACKNESS

'Lazarus?'

It was Arielle. Lazarus opened his mouth to reply, but nothing came out. He was having too much trouble battling wave after wave after wave of nausea and stomach cramps to even string a complete sentence together.

The angel helped him walk towards the shore. He'd been caught out, taken by surprise, but he was back now, and he knew exactly what had happened, what was so wrong. And now he was seriously pissed off at himself for missing it in the first place, ignoring it. But seeing his friend again had knocked him off track and sent his mind swimming.

He'd noticed it when they'd been walking out into the lake. When he'd first seen Abaddon, he'd had a sense something wasn't quite right. He'd felt the nausea. Why hadn't he done anything? What clearer sign did he ever need that the Dead were close? But he'd allowed himself to be distracted, to fob it off as nothing but a reaction to the water and the cold. It wouldn't happen again.

The water was ankle deep now. Arielle was still at his side, but Lazarus was no longer leaning on her. His strength had returned, and so had his focus. Ahead, he could see Abaddon striding out on to the shore, his heavy footsteps seeming to crush the ground beneath them. Still slung over his shoulder, and still unconscious, was Craig.

Lazarus held out a hand and pulled Arielle to a full stop.

'Can't you smell it?'

'You mean Abaddon? Of course I can. He always smells like that. Only worse now, thanks to where he's just been.'

Lazarus shook his head then pointed at Craig. 'No,' he said. 'Not Abaddon. Craig.'

'What about Cr—'

Arielle cut her sentence short and Lazarus saw that

the worst of all thoughts had ripped through her cranium like a tin opener.

'It's the Dead!' hissed Lazarus, his teeth clenched. 'He's occupied! And by something more powerful than I've ever experienced before.'

Arielle didn't look convinced. 'Are you sure?'

Lazarus nodded. 'Trust me on this.' But something else was bothering him. 'How come you or Abaddon didn't sense it and I did?'

Lazarus could tell Arielle was stumped. She shook her head, but at the same time her hand slipped to her sword. Lazarus followed suit, reaching down and yanking the spike out from his belt. He didn't notice the thorns on the handle any more, only the warmth of his own blood. It was a warmth that felt comforting, like his bleeding on the weapon was meant to be.

'I can't explain it,' said Arielle, her sword now free of its sheath. 'Are you absolutely sure?'

Before Lazarus had a chance to reply, a yell from the shore stabbed into them like a harpoon, and they both gasped.

Abaddon was on the ground, flat on his back. Astride

him was Craig. He was tearing into Abaddon, and no matter what the dead priest did, he couldn't stop the attack. Lazarus could see leathery flesh being pulled free, ripped from Abaddon's ribs and thrown aside.

Lazarus didn't wait for Arielle, and charged forward. He could hear Arielle behind him, then silence, as she leapt out of the water and landed beside Abaddon at the same time as Lazarus. Her sword was pinching Craig's neck and Lazarus knew it would take only a flick of her wrist to decapitate him and send his dead head spinning back into the lake.

Craig laughed then reached up to grip the blade of Arielle's sword. Instinctively, Arielle tried to snatch it away, but it wouldn't budge. Blood trickled from Craig's hand and Lazarus fully expected to see the sword blade sever his fingers. Instead, Craig snatched the weapon from Arielle's own hand, like a toy from a child, and flung it into the lake. Abaddon used the moment to try to struggle his way out, but Craig pinned him down hard. Then he leaned down to the side of his head, smiled and whispered. Lazarus tried to hear whatever it was Craig was muttering to Abaddon, but couldn't.

Craig sat up and laughed. And the heartbroken roar, which thrust its way out of Abaddon in response to what he'd just been told, was the sound of every parent screaming for a lost child.

A chill swept through Lazarus, bringing tears to his eyes. As he wondered what could make Abaddon screech so, Craig sat back up, winked at him, then flew into Abaddon with such a ferocious rain of punches that he almost turned away. Abaddon fell still and fought back no more.

'Craig!'

The name of his friend tore from Lazarus's throat like a stone wrapped in barbed wire.

Craig turned to face him, but it was not the face of his friend staring back. It was something so much darker that Lazarus half wondered if he was gazing into the very essence of evil, like liquid blackness had been poured into Craig, killing everything else. Whatever this thing was buried deep inside his friend, it had the power and strength to do something terrible. And he knew it had been sent for that very reason.

A horrible smile split Craig's cheeks forcing deep

lacerations to break his skin, covering his lips and chin in a bloody and clown-like grin. His eyes were wide and unblinking, and what was left of his clothing did little to cover the wounds across his body. He looked more like a corpse than the one he was sitting on and attacking.

Lazarus did everything he could to forget that this was his friend and focus on what was now residing inside him. He knew he had to rip out and send back to where it had come from. But it wasn't easy.

A gurgle slipped through the bleeding smile on the trail of a slick of blood that dribbled out like unwanted food.

'Hello, Keeper! Oh, how we have looked forward to meeting you! This is earlier than expected, thanks to your foolish dead friend here, but then perhaps so much the sweeter!'

Lazarus gripped the spike harder in his hand. Things were about to kick off any second now.

Craig nodded at Arielle, who now had her revolver aimed directly at his head.

'So this bitch is still hanging around Keepers like the stink she always was.'

It wasn't Craig talking. The voice sounded familiar, but it was warped and crushed, like every word was being pushed out through a ruined windpipe. And to hear words spat out with such venom by his friend disturbed Lazarus more than anything.

Craig looked at Arielle with eyes dripping disdain. 'Your name is mentioned most frequently, but then you know that.'

Arielle said nothing.

'Cat got your tongue? Or are you thinking about switching sides once again?'

Lazarus remembered what Arielle had said about her being a double-agent. It was unnerving to hear it talked about by one of the Dead.

It turned its gaze back to him.

'Lazarus, a word of advice. Trusting her? It would be hard to make a worse decision. She has betrayed before and she will do it again.'

It almost sounded like it actually cared. But more strange was the way it had referred to itself as 'we'.

Lazarus heard Arielle pull back the hammer on her revolver.

She wasn't serious . . .

'No!'

Arielle looked desperate. 'We have no choice, Lazarus! If I don't, this is where we lose; right here, right now! Don't you understand that?'

Craig laughed, or the thing inside him did. 'Sacrifice one for the good of the many? How very like you, Arielle.'

It laughed again and it sounded twisted and wrong. Then Craig clapped his hands together, almost in glee, before bringing a right hand hard across Abaddon's face.

'He's my friend!' Lazarus yelled out. 'You can't . . . you can't just kill him!'

'He's lost, Lazarus!' spat Arielle. 'You can't save him! To every war there are sacrifices! And that thing inside him? It doesn't just want you, it wants what's inside Abaddon! That's why it's here! That's why we haven't been attacked! It's all come down to this! We've been led here, herded like bloody sheep!'

Lazarus swayed, the moment almost swamped him.

'They knew we would come here,' continued Arielle,

her voice drenched in desperation. 'They knew Abaddon would go to the village. And that thing inside Craig has been sent back to put an end to us and to take the Black Shard! You have to listen to me!'

But Lazarus couldn't. His vision was blurry. Arielle was screaming at him, her revolver waving at Craig's head, but her voice was lost. Abaddon was barely moving. And Craig, the one friend he'd always been able to count on, was now the one person unwittingly at the very centre of everything crashing down about him. And that hideous, haunting grin cut across his face with all the tact of a chainsaw on full throttle.

Lazarus shook his vision clear just in time to see Craig punch his hand deep into Abaddon's chest then rip it back out, covered in black tar, and holding in its grasp the Black Shard.

Then he heard the gunshot.

16
WEEPING RED FLESH

Craig's head snapped back with such violence Lazarus could only think the worst had happened: the crazy angel had shot his brains out all over the shore. Smoke seeped from the revolver's barrel. But there was no blood.

For a second, Craig's head just hung there, like it was waiting to peel off at the neck and roll down his back.

Lazarus didn't realise he was holding his breath.

Craig's body shuddered. A ripple of movement raced up it, snapping his head forward with the sound of a whip crack. Then that laugh again, like a thousand hyenas being drowned.

Craig stood up, the Black Shard still in his hand, and looked at Arielle.

'Your shooting has not improved, Arielle.'

Arielle wasn't given time to reply as Craig brought the Black Shard round to slam her hard across the side of her head. Arielle tried to dodge, but the speed of it was astonishing and she crumpled to the ground with little more than a weak exhaled moan. Lazarus expected her to get straight back up. She didn't.

Lazarus called to his friend, even though he doubted that he could hear him.

Craig faced Lazarus, but someone else was staring out through those eyes. Lazarus had to keep that clear in his mind if he was going to stand any chance of doing what he was about to attempt.

'It is over, Keeper. Even your father has accepted his fate. So be a good boy and do the same.'

At the mention of his father, a rage so intense flared up inside Lazarus that every hair on his skin felt like it had scorched to a cinder.

'You do not speak of my father,' he snarled, teeth gritted.

'Touchy . . .'

Lazarus got a grip of himself. If he gave into the rage, he was lost for sure.

He breathed himself calm. 'I'm not listening to you. And I'm not talking to you either. I'm talking to Craig. The one whose body you stole. He's still in there and I know he can hear me. CRAIG!'

The Dead thing inside Craig rattled out another laugh, then spat a glob of blood down on to Abaddon, wiping a streak of red across his cheek.

'It is hopeless! Give up! We have this now!'

Craig held up the Black Shard, unwrapping it from the strip of leather that held it.

'Craig, I need your help,' said Lazarus, working hard to stay focused. 'Seriously, mate, we're in the shit unless you do something. I don't know how, but you have to try and fight it!'

Lazarus felt like an idiot talking to Craig as if he was somewhere else, when here he was, right in front of him.

Abaddon stirred only to receive a thick kick from Craig, delivered with enough force to roll him across the ground and into the lake, face down.

'Everything is coming together,' said Craig. 'You cannot win. Give up now.' It smiled like someone selling candy to kids. 'Why not join us?'

Lazarus shut that voice out. 'Craig! I'm not kidding around now – help me here!'

He hadn't a clue what he was expecting Craig to do. He was trapped in his own body, unable to do anything while the Dead thing that had taken it over used it as it desired.

Craig walked over to the unconscious Arielle. He used his foot to roll her over.

'We were telling the truth about this one, Lazarus. Do not trust her.'

'Craig – please!' Lazarus yelled out in one final attempt before he went on the offensive.

'You're not going to give up, are you, Keeper? What is the point? Can you not see this fight is futile?'

Lazarus raised the spike in his hand and pointed it at his friend. 'Get out of my friend now, before I rip you out!'

Craig laughed, but this time, it choked on itself. Lazarus saw a flicker of confusion and stepped forward. Was it Craig? Had he heard?

For a moment, Craig's body didn't move, just stayed its

ground, the Black Shard hanging suspended, frozen almost in his hand.

Craig spoke again, but this time it seemed to struggle to get the words out. 'You can't win, Keeper. Your father failed. You will fail too! Too many of us! Worse is to follow!'

But Lazarus wasn't listening. He'd had enough, not just of this conversation, but of feeling like he had no control over what was happening around him.

First, it had been his dad leaving him, thrusting him into this world of the Dead, of Hell and angels and demons. Then it had been his mother, coming back from the dead to try to destroy him. Now it was the Fallen.

From this moment on he was going to take the fight to who or whatever it was that was behind all this.

Craig raised the Black Shard.

'Dance with us, Keeper!'

And that was another thing Lazarus was sick of: people talking such total crap, soaking everything they said in phrases that sounded like cheesy lines in a bad movie.

Lazarus sprang at Craig, his spike gripped low. He was still hoping that he could save his mate and drag the Dead thing out of him; using the spike could put an end to that idea pretty sharpish. And to Craig.

Lazarus managed to grab a hold of him, dragging Craig down to the ground with him as he landed. The stones that stabbed his back went unnoticed, his body shut down to pain before his nerves had a chance to sing out.

Lazarus saw the Black Shard sweep round, ducked as it flew past his head, reached out to grab Craig's head, clamp it between his fingers, but was sent skywards. The thing inside Craig had a frightening strength and Lazarus landed hard. Again, he didn't register the pain, but was winded and it took him too long to get back to his feet. Craig was on the attack, kicking him back down as he tried to stand. Only this time, he wasn't just carrying the Black Shard; in his other hand was Arielle's sword. He must have grabbed it from the lake where it lapped against the shore.

The blade swiped past and Lazarus dropped to the ground. It came again, caught him in the arm, opening his flesh up like a fresh tomato. Blood splashed down.

Lazarus yelled out again: 'Craig!'

The sword came at him once more, but its trajectory

faltered, like someone had pulled at it with invisible thread. Lazarus spun left and drove himself at Craig's legs, dropping him like liquid. The sword clattered against the rocks on the shore. Craig yelled out, but the screams and shouts Lazarus heard were not of this world, dragged from some place much darker, somewhere extinguished of all hope.

He grabbed the hand holding the sword, fought back every instinct telling him that he was hurting his friend, was probably about to break a few of his bones in the process, may even have to kill him to survive this, and smashed it down until the sword fell free. Before Craig could respond, Lazarus slapped him hard across his face to stun him, then clamped his hands round his head.

Craig screamed as though Lazarus had rammed his head into a furnace.

Lazarus fought back tears as his friend started to buck and shake beneath him like he was being electrocuted, but he wasn't going to let go, not until this was finished. Not that he actually could; once the hands of a Keeper touched someone possessed by one of the Dead, they would only be released if the Dead thing was evicted.

Lazarus wanted to close his eyes, but couldn't. They refused to shut, like they wanted him to bear witness to what he was capable of, remember it always, a record of the horrors he was now not just a part of, but committing.

Craig's shaking grew more violent. His skin was burning, his screams filling the air with the sound of animals at the abattoir, cars crashing, machine guns blasting away the lives of millions, buildings collapsing, the world shattering into a million pieces . . .

It stopped.

Craig was still, his breathing sharp and shallow, like a dog panting. Lazarus wondered if it was over, but something told him the Dead thing was holding on.

He took a deep breath and stared down at his friend. Forcing himself to focus, he searched for the Dead thing in his friend, seeking it out with all of his mind, burrowing his own soul into Craig's, cutting through it to get to the infection like a surgeon's scalpel. If he tried to explain what he was doing, it would never make sense. It was just instinct, the Keeper inside him doing his job. At last he found it; a pulsing black stain clamped to Craig's spirit, sucking it dry, feeding off it. Without a second's hesitation, he hooked himself into it . . . and ripped it free!

Lazarus flew backwards with the force of what he'd done, cracking his head on a large stone. Sparks fizzed in front of his eyes. He slumped on to his side to hack up a great glob of phlegm choking his throat. Just away from him lay Craig, his chest barely moving; just enough to show that he was still breathing. Between them, lying half on the ground and half still somehow inside Craig, was the Dead.

Lazarus cried out involuntarily as the thing, impossibly large and clearly broken now, allowed its head, a swollen lump of weeping red flesh and charred bone, to roll to the side and stare at him. Its features were barely distinguishable. The fact Lazarus could tell that it was a head at all was simply because in the mass of pulsing, ruined meat and tissue, a mouth could be seen and a singular eye. But it wasn't singular, was it? No. It was like the eye of a spider; a thousand eyes together forming one giant, all-seeing, gelatinous orb. The mouth itself was little more than a hole filled with teeth that looked like they had just been poured in, and they clattered and rattled against each other with every movement the thing made. As for that hideous collection of eyes, they were all bloodshot to hell and with every blink a slender curtain of flesh would wipe the glistening, soft globe with a fresh veil of gore.

Lazarus took in the rest of the creature. Its torso was transparent and if there were organs inside it they seemed to churn round each other, jostling for position. Its arms were long and spindly, and they were pulling the thing forwards, dragging it out of Craig's body on a trail of foul-smelling sludge and slime, like an insect out of a cocoon.

A voice of pain called to Lazarus; it was Arielle.

'The Black Shard!'

Lazarus nodded, pushed himself to his feet. He raised the spike above his head, saw the creature, now at his feet, roll on to its back. It was, Lazarus thought, a pathetic thing. And what he was about to do wasn't simply necessary, but humane.

He steadied himself for the killing blow, when an immense black shadow swept from behind. Lazarus looked round to see something like a fighter jet crash down towards them. He ducked, felt it rush past, heard feathers. He looked up to see what it was, but the sky was empty.

A bubbling gurgle pulled Lazarus's attention back to the thing he'd been about to despatch. But something had got there first; the head was cleaved clean in two, spilling its insides on to the ground like a split, rotten watermelon. Its hands were severed; whatever had cut through the creature's head had sliced them clean off at the wrist. That got Lazarus's attention more than anything, because the hand that had held the Black Shard – which like the rest of the creature's body was dissolving into a thick, steaming soup – was empty.

'The Black Shard,' Lazarus said, his voice shaking as he looked from the melting body back to Arielle. 'It's gone!'

17
A FIERY METEOR

Arielle let out such a cry that Lazarus dropped the spike from his hands to cover his ears. It did little to stop the screech coursing through him with the power to scatter his soul amongst the stars. When Arielle's voice stilled, it was like all sound had been erased, and the pain of it made his ears hurt. He turned immediately to Craig.

'He's still breathing!'

Arielle didn't respond. She was on her knees, staring across the lake. At her side was Abaddon, his chest ripped as if a pack of wolves had mistaken him for lunch.

'He's still breathing, Arielle! Craig's alive!'

Still nothing.

'Arielle!'

'He would be better dead,' said Arielle finally. 'As

would we all. It is over, Lazarus. We have been played like fools!'

'Quit the drama and get over here,' Lazarus snapped back. Arielle could lose control if she wanted, but he wasn't about to. 'Now, Arielle!'

As she made her way over, Lazarus scanned the skies. Whatever had swooped at them must have taken the Black Shard, but he hadn't a clue where to start looking for it. If this was where everything was going to kick off, and if that sodding piece of rock was so important, it had to be close by.

It was while he was staring, that Lazarus heard something. At first, he thought it was the wind, and indeed it did seem to have picked up suddenly, but that wasn't it. He looked around, tried to place it, couldn't. Then something caught his eye. At first he thought he was making it up. But the more he stared the more he realised that his eyes weren't lying.

The sound was coming from the end of the wooden pier jutting out into the lake from the shore under the ruined church. The pier itself was empty, but in the water close to the very end of it, was the source.

Lazarus almost shook his head in disbelief: a huge whirlpool was pulling the lake into it, and it was spinning so ferociously that the pier itself was shaking and Lazarus found himself almost hoping to see the thing rip out and get torn up by the maelstrom. This was the same whirlpool Matthew had filmed.

'Laz?'

Craig's voice drew Lazarus away from the whirlpool and he spun round to see his mate sitting up, rubbing his brow like he was recovering from a hangover.

'You look like shit.'

'Odd that,' replied Craig, wincing with pain. 'Where are we? What happened?'

'What do you remember?'

For a moment, Craig was silent. He sounded tired as much as anything.

When he looked back up his eyes were lifeless, terrified by the memory of the things they had seen, things Lazarus knew they still saw, played over and over.

'I remember everything,' said Craig. 'So many of them, Laz! Not just one, but *dozens* inside me!'

Craig was shaking and as panic tore through him he

leapt at Lazarus, burrowing himself into his chest with a desperate cry.

Lazarus nearly lost it completely right then, and he wrapped his arms round his friend to steady him. To see and hear Craig look and sound so lost and haunted was too much. None of this should've been Craig's business in the first place; he shouldn't even be here! He pushed back tears; now was not the time.

A screech, like the call of a bird of prey, slashed the moment in two and caused them to look up to the sky. They all saw it; the distant silhouette of wings. Lazarus didn't need to be told what it was; it was the Fallen one from the moor, and in its hand was the Black Shard.

It dropped from the sky like a fiery meteor, streaking down to the lake with such suddenness Lazarus threw himself and Craig to the ground. It sped down and into the lake, right into the whirlpool at the end of the pier. And behind it, shooting up and out into the sky, was an explosion of steam.

'Bastard!' muttered Arielle as Abaddon stirred. 'Made sure we were all watching!'

The dead priest shivered and sat up. He stared at his empty chest cavity, pulled the shredded remains of his clothes and coat over it and stood up.

'The Shard is gone,' said Arielle despairingly.

Abaddon said nothing.

'Did you not hear me, Abaddon? It's gone! We're screwed! Why the hell didn't you tell me about the shard before? Why? You selfish, dead idiot!'

Abaddon regained his composure, but something about him was different.

Lazarus remembered the scream, Craig whispering . . .

'Abaddon?'

The living corpse turned to face him.

'Craig whispered something to you. What was it?'

At this, Arielle swept round on Lazarus. 'What are you talking about?'

Abaddon was silent.

'You screamed,' Lazarus continued to question. 'Something that makes someone like you make a noise like that must've been pretty bloody serious, right?'

Abaddon went to say something, but faltered.

'Abaddon? What did that thing inside Craig say to

you?' Lazarus heard not just fear and despair, but concern in Arielle's voice.

One word slipped from Abaddon's cracked and broken mouth: 'Mary . . .'

Arielle flickered her eyes at Lazarus. 'Things might just be about to get a whole lot worse.'

Abaddon took a tentative step and stumbled. Arielle went to help him but he shook her off angrily.

'Leave me be, angel.'

'You're weak.'

Abaddon responded with a grunt and kept walking, making his way slowly past Lazarus and back to the Defender.

Watching his slow progress, Lazarus asked, 'What did it tell you?'

Abaddon stopped. 'That Mary is still alive, Lazarus!'

Arielle jumped at this. 'You know that's impossible, right?' she said. 'And even if she is, what do you think you can do? If the Dead inside her has kept her body living and breathing all this time, they will be too intertwined.'

Lazarus didn't understand. 'How do you mean?'

Abaddon paused. 'Too long joined with the Dead and the body cannot survive without it,' he said. 'If we evicted the Dead from Mary, she would die. Her body would age in moments. She would be gone.'

Lazarus didn't want to guess at what Abaddon was feeling now, but he could hear something terrible in his voice and it frightened him.

'You can do nothing for her,' said Arielle dismissively. 'You don't even know if what you heard was lies to distract you! The Dead know your weakness, Abaddon; do not let them exploit it!'

'Nothing?' said Abaddon, disdain dripping from his lips. 'You really think that releasing Mary is nothing?'

'That is not what I said!'

Abaddon sniffed at Arielle and approached Lazarus.

'I will have my vengeance, Keeper; do not stand in my way.'

A laugh cut the moment and Lazarus saw Arielle, hipflask at her lips. She tipped it up and sank the liquid with a gulp.

'I'm sure that'll help.'

Arielle turned her dead eyes on to Lazarus. 'The Black

Shard is gone, Lazarus.' She took another hit from the flask. 'And with it what little hope we ever had!' She shook her head. 'No vengeful priest can help us now. Not even the Keeper! Not with the Fallen approaching. How could I have been so foolish? I have led us to this! All along I should have foreseen it, but I saw nothing! NOTHING!'

Another drink, but it didn't last long. With reactions and accuracy Lazarus had never known he possessed, he'd catapulted his spike to snatch the hipflask out of Arielle's hand and pinned it to the ground.

Arielle applauded. Slowly.

Lazarus retrieved the spike, then walked towards the Defender. Arielle was rubbing her head, like she was trying to erase a headache. Abaddon was now at the rear of the truck, a haunted look on his leathery face as he retrieved his weapons.

'Where are you going?'

The voice was Craig's and when Lazarus stopped to look over at his friend, he saw a loyalty in his eyes that almost slayed him. His wounds seemed less violent now, as if they had been there because of the Dead thing inside him. He was exhausted but his eyes were bright and alive.

'Where that thing went,' replied Lazarus, and pointed out across the lake with the spike. 'The whirlpool is a rupture in the veil. And at its very bottom is the village, right, Abaddon?'

Abaddon nodded as he placed yet another flintlock into a hidden loop inside his jacket.

'You cannot get there,' he said. 'It is impossible. It was never a part of the plan to have you wander in that place. It is I who must go.'

Lazarus threw his hands up in the air in disbelief. 'Don't take the piss, Abaddon! For a start there's more to this than just you and Mary, OK?'

Abaddon snarled. 'Says the boy who only ever whines about his father, like a little runt of a puppy kicked from the litter's warm bed!'

Lazarus's blood hit boiling point.

'Don't push me, Abaddon!'

'Just stay out of my way, Keeper.'

'And as for a plan? We've been making this up as we go along! And we're bloody lucky to have survived this far!'

'That matters not,' said Abaddon. 'Simmerdale is not just at the bottom of the lake. It is deeper than that, at the very bottom of this world! You cannot go.'

Lazarus wasn't listening. He'd seen where the fallen angel had gone and he had no choice but to follow. He certainly wasn't going to sit around waiting for the end of all things like a commercial break on TV.

Catching sight of Arielle rising to her feet, he turned and continued on towards the Defender. He soon heard a scrabbling of stone and the sound of feet trying to catch him up. When he turned it wasn't Arielle like he'd expected.

It was Craig.

'I'm coming with you.'

18
UNFINISHED BUSINESS

Lazarus's heart jumped. Those were words he wanted to hear, but he couldn't take Craig with him, not after all he'd gone through.

'Don't be an idiot.'

'I'm not,' said Craig, and Lazarus heard his determination and refusal to take no as an answer.

'I've been there. I know the place. It was where Clair and I were taken. It's like some kind of holding post for the Dead so that they can slip through. I don't really know how it works. But I've been there, Laz; I'll be useful!'

'It's still no,' said Lazarus, desperate to say yes, but every part of him telling him it's wrong, Craig can't come. 'Not after what you've been through. You're injured.'

'After what I've been through I have to, Laz! Don't you see that? I can't just sit back here and pretend I'm trying to recover, when everything I've seen . . . felt . . .'

Craig's voice broke.

'Look, I know what you're saying, I know why,' said Lazarus. 'But I can't allow it.'

'Don't you dare leave me here, Laz, OK? You need me. You know it. You can't just go walking in there without a map!'

'Then draw me one.'

Craig tapped his head. 'It's all up here, mate. I'm your veritable living satnav!'

There it was; Craig's ability to throw a serious conversation off bar with a funny at the end. Lazarus couldn't fight the smile.

'I'm not going anywhere with someone who uses the word veritable . . .'

The warmth of the smile spread quickly, but it still wasn't enough and Lazarus attempted to make off again. But Craig's hand stalled him and he snapped round, fire in his eyes.

'I know the village, mate. That thing inside me knew the place. I can still sense it, walk round it in my head as if I lived there! And believe me when I say it's not a place you want to go alone, even if you have got that sick-looking spike bursting out all over your hand like the world's worst ever piercing.'

'He's right, Laz. You know it.' Arielle's voice chipped in.

'And how's that?'

'You can't take me, I'm too obvious. May as well just walk in there with a big sign saying *Kill Me Now*.'

'What about Abaddon? He seems keen.'

'He stays here with me.'

'And why should I do that, angel?' Abaddon growled.

It was a sound that made Lazarus believe that even without the Black Shard inside him, Abaddon would still be like taking on a Sherman tank in a fist-fight. Even more so now that he knew about his daughter.

'Because,' said Arielle, coming over to join them, 'I think that our best hope lies in Lazarus. As it always did.'

'Hang on,' said Lazarus. 'Where's all your despair gone? All that crap about losing the Black Shard and no one being able to help any more? I thought you'd given up.'

'Momentary blip,' replied Arielle, like nothing had happened. 'Even angels feel like giving up occasionally.'

Abaddon checked a pistol and said, 'I'm not staying

with you. I have unfinished business.'

'I know,' said Arielle, slipping her sword from its scabbard. 'And I think that business lies up there.' She nodded towards the commune then back to Lazarus. 'Take Craig while it's all still fresh in his mind and you'll have a better chance at whatever it is you think you can accomplish. I will stay here with Abaddon.'

'And do what?' answered the priest.

With barely a flicker of her eyes at Lazarus, Arielle told Abaddon about the girl they had seen just before Matthew's camper van exploded.

'It was Lazarus who spotted it,' said Arielle. 'The family resemblance. I didn't want to believe it, but after what that thing in Craig told you . . .'

'Then she is here? My Mary?'

Arielle gave a nod but was back to Lazarus. 'Her presence here bodes badly, Lazarus. What is now occurring has been in the making for lifetimes. We will do what we can, but you must now truly become the Keeper, perhaps even the last!'

'But I don't know what I'm doing! You know that, right?'

Arielle winked. 'Then whatever you do will take our enemies by surprise, won't it?'

'You sure about this?' Lazarus said.

'No,' said Craig. 'But it's not going to make any difference, and you know it. Clair's still there somewhere. Your dad.' He winked. 'And without me, how are you going to ever see the funny side of all this?'

Lazarus at last allowed that faint earlier smile to take over. And even though every fibre in his body was telling him to force Craig to stay with Arielle and Abaddon, he grinned widely, 'Come on then.'

Craig fell into step next to Lazarus at which point Arielle called over, 'Just out of interest, exactly how are you going to get to Simmerdale? You didn't seem that keen on using the diving equipment when I last asked.'

Lazarus said nothing as he climbed into the driver's seat of the Defender. He jammed the spike between the front seats and found the keys in the ignition. 'Just because you're an angel doesn't mean that you're impervious to crime!' he shouted to Arielle, waving the keys at her.

'And being the Keeper doesn't mean you can't die!'

Arielle retorted. 'Answer me: how are you going to get to the village?'

Craig heaved himself into the passenger seat. Lazarus fired up the engine and saw a faint ripple of pain flicker in his friend's face. He reached over and pulled from the nearest cupboard an old jumper, and threw it at Craig, along with some chocolate.

'You're absolutely sure about this?'

Craig pulled the sweater on, clicked in his seat belt, and pushed the chocolate into his mouth.

'I'll take that as a yes.'

A dark silhouette appeared at Craig's window making them both jump. It was Abaddon.

He reached out and held Craig's arm. 'Here,' he said, slipping something out from inside his coat. 'Lazarus has the spike, but you will need some form of protection also.'

Craig took what Abaddon was handing him; it was a pair of deadly-looking scythes.

'Thanks, I think,' said Craig, holding the blades in front of him like they were about to slice him in two.

'We'll be back as soon as we can,' said Lazarus.

'If you return at all it will be a miracle,' said Arielle

now at Abaddon's side. 'If you find the Black Shard, Lazarus, destroy it. The Dead and the Fallen will still come, but it will buy us time. It will loosen their hold on the rupture in the veil. But more than that, I cannot say.'

Without another word, Lazarus pushed into first gear and accelerated just hard enough to spin out a flurry of pebbles from the beach. He tried not to think about it, but he couldn't help wondering – if they returned would Abaddon still be around?

'Two questions,' said Craig, as Lazarus swung the Defender on to the road and started to head back up the way they had come. 'One, when did you learn to drive? And two, how are we going to get back to the village? It's not like it's signposted down a nice country lane.'

Lazarus answered through action only. He rammed the truck into second and spun the thing forwards, heaving it left. Water and pebbles flew as they crashed into the waves lapping the shore, sped past Arielle and Abaddon, and were at the wreckage of the mobile home. Lazarus leapt out and was back in a flash.

Craig looked at what Lazarus was carrying. 'I don't reckon this is the best time to be starting a new hobby, mate.'

Lazarus dumped Matthew's diving kit on the seat between him and Craig. It was an air cylinder with a mouthpiece attached to it by a black hose. He had no idea how to use it, but it was the best chance they had for where he was about to take them.

He pulled the Defender back round and bounced it out of the parking area on to the road.

After barely a couple of minutes Lazarus saw the entrance gate to the commune ahead. He dabbed the brakes, dropped a gear, pulled round and charged through, then skidded to a halt. Directly ahead, he saw that the road they'd come in on led neatly through the site, past the ruined church and to the pier. Across the water he could see the festival sparking into life. It was evening now, and the lights from the stage danced in the sky like a shattered rainbow scattered by the wind. More than that, though, sitting in that commune, he could sense death everywhere, like it was seeping from the very ground beneath them. He couldn't see anyone walking around the place, but he just knew, out of instinct, and because of that hideous sense that he was on the verge of puking, that every single person here – wherever they were hiding – was occupied. And not one of them had any idea that a pissed-off angel with a bellyful of whisky, and a dead priest armed to the teeth, were at that very moment on their way.

Craig knocked Lazarus from his thoughts. 'What are we doing?'

Lazarus took the mouthpiece for the air cylinder, fiddled with the thing attaching it to the cylinder, tried it and heard a hiss. Against all the odds, the thing was working! Were things about to start going his way?

'Take this,' he said, handing the mouthpiece to Craig. 'We're just going to have to try and swap the air supply as we go, until we get there.'

'I don't understand,' Craig replied. 'We're in a Land Rover Defender and now you're telling me we're going diving?'

Lazarus said nothing, just pushed the mouthpiece into Craig's mouth, and floored it.

Some twenty-two seconds later, the Defender crashed through the railing lining the platform at the end of the pier doing exactly sixty-seven miles an hour.

19
RIPPED EARTH

The Defender hit the spinning sides of the whirlpool with all the grace and finesse of a rhino leaping off a diving board. The front end was caught in the current and swung violently round, whipping the rest of the vehicle into the water with a deafening slam. Lazarus's head cracked against the door window. He saw the mouthpiece knocked from Craig, watched him grab for it, swearing his head off, then water rushed into the cabin and he closed his eyes.

In his own darkness, Lazarus saw the last few moments when the whirlpool had opened like the mouth of a starving whale beneath them, as they'd raced off the end of the pier. In that split second before the Defender had crashed down into the lake, he'd had no second thoughts breaking through his skull. It may have been a crazy decision, but it was the only one he could have made.

A hand knocked against him. Craig was staring at him, the mouthpiece firmly in place. His eyes were wide in terror, but when Lazarus reached out and held his friend's hand, he felt it gripped with such firm resolve he knew Craig was still with him. If reassurance were possible in such insane circumstances, that's what Lazarus felt.

The spinning of the whirlpool, which was gaining speed, pushed them back in their seats with increasing force. It was like being on a nightmare rollercoaster, but this wasn't a ride where you knew at the end you'd just get off and go buy some candyfloss.

Water splashed over both of them as the cabin filled up. Soon they'd be completely submerged.

Craig's voice forced its way through the hellish sound of the swirling water and the damage it was doing to the Defender, like it was trying to tear it to shreds.

'Here! Take a breath!'

Lazarus took the mouthpiece, filled his lungs deep, handed it back. The Defender was upended and sucked down with such speed that what air was still in the cabin was pushed out in an instant.

The Defender accelerated. It was like being on a jet as it launched itself down the runway. Except here, they weren't about to take off and fly through a nice clear sky, they were on a watery highway to Hell. *God, what had he done . . .*

The spinning continued. Lazarus had his eyes shut, couldn't think, couldn't breathe. Something knocked into him. He pushed it away. It knocked again. He remembered Craig had the air supply, grabbed at the mouthpiece, breathed deep. The oxygen tasted almost too clean, and it felt utterly at odds with normality to breathe underwater. It brought the reality of the situation home to him like a slap across the face. He gulped more air, his heart raced, he pushed the mouthpiece back to Craig, opened his eyes . . . and immediately wished that he hadn't.

The water was clear. He could see it rushing past outside the Defender, filled with bubbles like a hail of diamonds, but inside it was still, like they were sinking trapped inside a giant glass sphere. Directly in front of him, the water was a spinning vortex ending in a black dot getting closer and closer. He had no idea what speed they were doing, but it was horribly quick. And they were still accelerating.

Matthew hadn't been lying about the depth of the lake; they'd have hit the bottom just seconds after racing off the end of the pier, but they'd been in the whirlpool for what seemed like an age.

Then, as Lazarus fought to keep his mind sane against everything that was being thrown at it, the black dot he'd seen far off exploded outwards, crashing up through the water until it engulfed them completely.

Lights out . . .

Lazarus spluttered, and water sped out of his lungs. He leaned forward to puke it out of his mouth on to his lap. Eyes still closed, he leaned back, gasped for breath. He coughed again, but only dribbles came up this time. But if he thought that was it, he was wrong.

Wherever they'd ended up, Lazarus's mouth tasted like he'd taken a fat bite out of a rancid steak. The reek and taste and texture of where they were slipped into him uninvited and with such intimacy that his whole body felt violated. His skin crawled, he shivered, his stomach churned and his nerves sung out like he'd fallen into a coffin filled with pins.

Lazarus searched hard and deep for something inside himself to hold on to and stop himself passing out, drowning in this sudden sea of disease and death and rot and mould and decay. An image of his dad floated into his mind and he reached for it, drank it in, let it slip through him until he was back in control.

At last, and, with more than a little hesitation, he allowed his eyes to fall open. He half expected to be attacked in the same way again, to not be able to fight back, but thankfully he had that under control.

Oddly relieved, the first thing Lazarus noticed was that they were the right way up. The Defender was on its wheels and he could hear water still slipping out of it on to the ground below. Even more amazingly, the engine was still ticking over.

Outside, it was dark, but not so very much that he couldn't make out shapes some way off from them: buildings. Lazarus remembered Abaddon's description of where the village lay; the black lands, he had called it. It was easy to see why. The darkness outside the Defender wasn't just that caused by lack of sunlight. This was a darkness created by a lack of everything; light and life and whatever lay in between. It was thick and heavy and as Lazarus stared into it, he was almost convinced he could see the stuff move, like it was breathing. Then he noticed something else; a weird-looking machine with a propeller and a smashed camera. It was Matthew's submersible, he realised. So this was what had happened to it!

Another cough and Lazarus turned to face Craig. He was going through the same motions, vomiting up the water, trying to work out how they'd survived.

'Hey,' said Lazarus.

Craig raised a hand. 'Hey.'

'Quite a ride.'

A nod. Another cough.

Lazarus waited till Craig was back in control. He was pleased to have him along, but he was still finding it hard to deal with the responsibility of bringing him back here in the first place.

'It's always an adventure, being your mate,' said Craig, wiping his mouth and turning to Lazarus.

Lazarus unclipped his seatbelt. The sopping strap took some persuading to slip back into its reel. He tapped a finger on the windscreen.

'Recognise this place?'

Craig stared out to what Lazarus was pointing at and nodded.

'Can't say I'm happy to be back.'

'I didn't want you to come at all.'

'I know,' said Craig and opened his door.

'Wait!' said Lazarus a little louder than he meant to. 'We don't know what's out there yet!'

Craig slipped out of the Defender, Abaddon's scythes gripped in his hands, and said, 'Actually, I do.'

Lazarus switched off the engine, slipped the keys into his pocket, then jumped out and walked round to meet Craig at the front of the Defender. The scythes suited him, but in a bad way. Craig was one of those people who was supposed to always look and be happy, as if no matter what the world did, no matter how bad things got, he would always see the positive. But now, standing so terribly armed, covered in the wounds of what he'd endured at the hands of the Dead, Lazarus knew his friend had changed. What worried him most was that he had no idea how different Craig really was. And, if things kicked off, and those scythes started whirring, what he would become. He could sense a darkness in his friend now. It was unnerving.

Lazarus forced a smile to his face. The air was still and smelled damp and if he'd thought he'd be able to dry off by walking around a bit, he'd been wrong. It was raining. Not hard, but constant and miserable.

'That's the village,' said Craig, pointing off through the dreary, damp gloom to the shadowy shapes Lazarus had spotted. 'Just out of interest, how long was I there before Abaddon found me? And why does this place stink so bad? It's like we've landed close to a fish factory that's been shut down and left to rot in the sun!'

Lazarus didn't respond; he knew Craig wasn't expecting an answer. A place like this, sitting halfway between the bottom of a lake and Hell? It was going to stink, it was just a case of how bad. As for the other question? 'Just two days,' he replied. 'Feels like two years.'

'Mum's going be seriously pissed that I've not called.'

'If it's any consolation, I'm guessing the signal here's pretty bad.'

Craig laughed. It was a good sound, thought Lazarus, but it jarred with the surroundings and seemed to bounce around looking for a way to escape until it finally gave up and fizzled out.

'So what now?'

It was the question Lazarus had been dreading. He walked back round to his door, reached in, and returned to Craig with the spike in his hand. Now they were both ready.

He pointed his spike towards what Craig had said was the village.

'Something called the Black Shard was ripped from Abaddon's chest,' he said, deciding mid-sentence not to give away the fact that it was Craig who had committed the deed. 'We need to find it and destroy it.'

'And you're sure it's down here, right? We haven't just come here on a sightseeing trip.'

Lazarus continued. 'The thing that took it; we followed it down that whirlpool.' His shoulders dropped under the weight of what he'd just said. 'What the crap are we doing, Craig?'

'Saving the world, mate.'

'It was a rhetorical question.'

'My favourite.'

Lazarus said no more, just gripped the spike harder and set off walking. With each step, the shadows ahead grew more clear, until out of the endless rain, they appeared together, like a smudged watercolour painting of a pastoral countryside scene. Except it was the nightmare version, the kind of painting that would never see light of day on the wall of any gallery.

Lazarus knew they were stepping back in time. Simmerdale, cursed by the priest who had served it, had last seen daylight centuries ago. And as they came upon the outskirts of that haunted place, it was like walking on to a film set.

The place sat silent and eerie in front of them, like it had been ripped from its resting place and dropped on to the surface of the moon. Stretching left and right, slipping around the village perimeter like a barrier, a ridge of land rose upwards, formed of torn and ripped earth. It rose above them in places, and in others had slumped and crumbled to little more than a very gradual slope leading up to the village. In places, the ends of walls could be seen, tumbles of rocks and rubble frozen in a time, spilling on to the dark plain Lazarus and Craig were stood on.

Thin watery rivulets cut down through the earth, fed continuously by the endlessly falling rain. They made it look like the place was wounded and bleeding, lying in its death throes, but never being allowed to fully die.

Lazarus spotted an easy place to walk up on to the earthen ridge. It was clearly the old road that had once led into the village, and he and Craig climbed up, scrabbling their feet over a mix of old cobbles, mud and stone, which had lain quiet and unused for so very long. Jutting out of the ground to the left of the ruined remains of the road, was a carved stone.

'Simmerdale,' read Craig, leaning down to look at the stone.

But it wasn't that which drew Lazarus's attention. It was the neat set of footprints he saw in the road ahead, leading off towards the village.

20

SEEPING DARKNESS

'Is it me, or does it look like someone just dropped out of the sky?'

Lazarus, like Craig, was looking down at the footprints sunk into the ground in front of them. They were large, like those of a basketball player's, but the proportions seemed utterly perfect. Flawless. Each print showed a detailed relief from toe to heel, like a small inverted map of valleys and streams. The prints sat shoulder-width apart, and were in the mud deep. Leading with the left foot, they headed off into the village.

Craig knelt down to look at the prints more closely. He glanced around, clearly trying to find something, then stood back up. 'Definitely not another print in sight,' he said, 'except these, and all they do is lead on up to the village. Whoever made these either fell out of the sky or they jumped a hell of a long way from somewhere else.'

Lazarus's only thought was that these had to be the footprints of the Fallen they'd seen shoot out of the sky and into the whirlpool. They had unfinished business . . .

'Well?' said Craig.

'Is this where I'm supposed to act all leader-like and outline my great and detailed plan?'

Craig nodded.

'What a shitter.'

'So we just wing it then?'

'Looks that way.'

Lazarus, despite his current predicament, was almost enjoying himself, though perhaps *enjoy* was too strong a word. Having Craig back made him realise just how much he'd missed having him around. Arielle wasn't one for seeing the funny side, and as for Abaddon? He seemed blessed with the ability to suck not just the joy out of the moment, but the light out of the day. He was a big walking hole of darkness and foreboding, and talking to him was like staring down a well to shout your name, then getting creeped out by the echo.

A sound came from ahead, like something heavy being dragged through a puddle.

'It's that kind of thing that doesn't make me all that keen on going any further,' said Lazarus, flicking his eyes to where the sound came from. 'A sound like that's bound to have something horrible at the end of it. And it probably wants to rip our guts out.'

'Then it's a good job I'm here,' said Craig. 'With these.'

He raised the scythes so that they framed his face.

'Just make sure if and when you have to use them, I'm nowhere near you.'

Craig gave a faint nod and Lazarus, gripping the spike harder than ever, moved forwards, following the solitary trail of footprints to the village.

The walk was short, but to Lazarus felt longer and longer with each step as though the village was trying to repel them. It was a struggle to put one foot in front of the other. The effort made him sweat. Because of the rain, Craig didn't notice. But what was going on? Was it the village? Was there something in it that didn't want him turning up for a nosy? Or was he just making it up? Lazarus didn't know, but was relieved when they at last passed the first building and were able to stand and stare along the singular street that was Simmerdale. The sense of being pushed away faded, like they'd been walking against the wind all that time, only to have it suddenly die on them.

'Where do we start?' asked Craig. 'Do we just knock from door to door until we find whoever it is that nicked the rock and ask for it back?'

'Abaddon found you in one of the houses, being prepared for something by the Dead,' said Lazarus. 'Don't suppose you remember which one?'

Craig's silence was answer enough.

Lazarus stared at Simmerdale, allowed his eyes to creep along the grey road that divided the two rows of simple, stone houses and other buildings from each other, wondering just how such a place could exist at all. Simmerdale, he realised, would always be the kind of place that reached out to you to tear your still-beating heart from your breast. It was not just a village between worlds. It was something much, much worse. And it was all Lazarus could do to stay on his feet, as a hush of wind washed over him with the stench of the Dead.

Fighting with everything he had against the need to vomit, he squeezed his eyes shut, clenched his fists. He wasn't going to give in to it, not here, not now. He was the Keeper; he had to stay in control and not let what was happening to him control him instead.

A hand rested on his shoulder.

'You OK? You look like you need to sit down.'

'Fine, I'm just fine,' Lazarus replied, but made good use of the added support of Craig to regain his strength. It didn't take long, but it was still a horrible sensation. He wondered if he'd ever get used to it. Probably not. And he wondered how his dad had learned to deal with it, and keep it secret, too.

Head cleared, Lazarus gritted his teeth and took his first step into Simmerdale, his eyes wide with the horror of the place, and every sense he had on full alert for something to come crashing down upon them, teeth and claw.

The awfulness of Simmerdale only really became apparent to Lazarus once he'd taken those first steps through its outer boundary. The place sat under a thick darkness, which seemed to sag over the houses like a huge, plastic tarpaulin holding back a torrent of water, and just waiting to burst. In places it came so low that only half of a house was visible, or it sat slumped across a roof like it was resting on it for a while. Everywhere was a soaked, sopping, dripping mess. Water ran freely down the brickwork of the houses. It slipped out from under doors, wept down the shutters clamped hard across blind windows, and gurgled and bubbled into the street, seeping in between the cobbles, pooling in some places, flowing in little black, brown streams in others. As they walked down the street, Lazarus tried to see into the houses, but the places were locked down. And the little alleyways that ran off here and there were filled with that seeping darkness; if anything was hiding in it, Lazarus just couldn't see.

At the other end of the village Lazarus saw a graveyard. He remembered Abaddon saying it was where he'd buried the Black Shard, at the graves of his family.

'What's to see there?' asked Craig, following on behind.

Lazarus explained about Abaddon's family. 'Figured we might find a clue or something.'

But he figured wrong. The place, like Simmerdale itself, was a dead end to nothing. He found gravestones, but had no idea which were Abaddon's family. And nothing about the place told him anything about the village. But then why should it have? He'd come here on a whim as much as anything; expecting to find something was just asking too much.

Lazarus turned round to leave the graveyard and head back through Simmerdale but stopped short of taking a step.

'Laz?' said Craig, clearly seeing the look of horror on his friend's face. 'What's up?'

Laz said nothing, just grabbed Craig and pulled him down behind a large gravestone.

'What the hell?'

Lazarus hushed Craig and pointed through the gravestones into the village. 'Something's kicking off,' he said.

'What?'

Lazarus didn't answer, and instead peeked out from

where they were hiding.

All along each side of the road leading through the village, he could see doors opening and people flooding out. But these weren't ordinary people.

These were the actual Dead.

They completely blocked the road. From one of the houses, something was carried out and across the Dead by clawing hands. It was a body tied up with rope and wire, and gagged. Lazarus knew in an instant that this was someone who was neither one of the Dead nor yet occupied by them. Whoever it was, they were struggling, but it was doing them no good; whichever way they twisted or turned, a hand would find them, keep them on track to wherever it was they were being sent.

For a moment Lazarus tried to second-guess where the victim was being taken, wondering if he could get there first, help. But he soon changed his mind when he saw, slipping out from one of the dark alleyways, something that he recognised. It was a wooden frame, held high by a number of the Dead. The person who had been crowd-surfed in terror across those awful, clawing hands, was brought towards it.

'Laz,' said Craig, his voice soft and scared, 'why am I getting déjà vu?'

'Because,' replied Lazarus, 'this is what we saw happen to my dad.'

Lazarus dropped down behind the gravestone as he heard the person start to scream. He squeezed his eyes shut, pushed his fists into them to fill his head with sparks and stars and explosions, but it did no good; he could still see a perfect recording of what had happened to his dad. The Dead had taken him, strapped him to a frame like the one they'd just seen, then filled him with darkness. And he had become a weapon of the Dead: the Dark, something that, if released in the land of the Living, could snuff out the light on humanity and allow the Dead to swarm in, take over. All the Dead had to do was get it to the other side, and this village was the bridge they needed. But it was worse than that now. The Fallen were involved. Hell was at hand.

The sound of wings brought Lazarus back.

'What's happening?'

Craig peered round the gravestone. 'They've strapped the person to that frame,' he said. 'I think it's a man – no,

I'm sure it is; the ginger beard is pretty obvious.'

That description made Lazarus whip round.

'It's Matthew,' he said, horrified. 'And he's alive . . .'

21
HALF DEAD

'Who's Matthew?'

'He discovered the whirlpool,' said Lazarus.

'So how's he here?' Craig asked.

Lazarus was about to say he hadn't the faintest idea, but then he remembered something about the commune and the ruined church, the pier . . .

He'd seen the people at the commune throwing stuff off the end of the pier, hadn't he? And at the time he'd figured it was nothing more than some weird pseudo-religious baptism thing. But then he and Arielle had learned, thanks to Matthew's discovery, that the strange whirlpool sat right under it. A connection hadn't occurred to him at the time, probably because he'd been so focused on Craig turning up, but now? And after seeing that Fallen angel dive into it?

The truth hit him hard. People were being thrown off the pier, into the whirlpool, to be sent to Simmerdale, and to the Dead! The thought chilled him. It meant that the Dead and the Fallen were running the place, setting things up for what was to come: *Hell.* Lazarus remembered Abaddon's daughter. What if she had been the first, sent through to get things started? Perhaps that was what Arielle had meant when she had spoken of everything now having been in the making for lifetimes?

He knew that the last splash he'd seen, the one that had caught his attention as he'd been wading out to meet Abaddon bringing Craig out of the lake, had been Matthew. It had to be. But why send people into the whirlpool to end up down here?

'You need to see this, Laz,' said Craig, interrupting Lazarus's train of thought. 'They're doing to Matthew what I remember them doing to me.'

Craig's voice cut off with a broken cry and he fell back into Lazarus. He looked like he'd just witnessed his own murder.

'Still with me?'

Craig nodded. 'I can't watch. I can't go through that again.'

Lazarus stared back into the village. Matthew was hanging high above the crowd of the Dead. A large space had cleared in front of him, and standing in it was the fallen angel. Held aloft in his right hand was the Black Shard. But it was twice the size now; this wasn't just the piece from Abaddon, it was now attached to its other half, the piece that had sent Simmerdale to Hell.

The angel was speaking to the crowd in a language Lazarus didn't understand. The voice was menacing, but at the same time musical and lilting, and seemed at moments to slip through the air with the ease and grace of an eagle, only to be pulled out of it with a snarl that chewed the sound up and spat it back out, mangled and wrong. And it would use the Black Shard to point out across and over where Lazarus and Craig were hiding.

Lazarus turned expecting to see something worth pointing at, but it was all just more impenetrable darkness. Then he caught sight of something far off, almost too faint for him to notice: a light. It seemed light years away, but burned with such an intensity that it made Lazarus turn from it, blinking away the image of it like a photo negative behind his eyes.

The fallen angel was silent. The Dead fell into an absolute frenzy, ripping at themselves, leaping into the air, into each other. Some tripped to the ground to be crushed, others were thrown upwards, and some were pulled apart in the mayhem. It was a violence that Lazarus felt would soon spill their way, wash over them and drown them in a sea of rot and bile. But amazingly, it stayed contained, the crowd content to pile into and on top of each other again and again, rather than trying to escape.

Craig was still staring at the figure holding the Black Shard. 'He's huge!'

'He's one of the Fallen,' explained Lazarus. 'An angel sent to Hell?'

'How do you know?'

'He's tried to kill me,' said Lazarus. 'Twice.'

The fallen angel lifted itself into the air, its wings hardly moving. It slipped through the air to Matthew, who ceased his struggling, like all his fight had been quashed in an instant. For a moment, it simply hung there, staring at him, then in a flash of movement it grabbed two of the

Dead from the crowd and slung them at Matthew.

Matthew screamed. It sounded like every atom in his body was responding in shock.

Lazarus stumbled backwards.

The Dead hit Matthew and sunk into his body, like pins into jelly. Matthew's body convulsed, blood burst from his mouth and gushed from his eyes and ears. He yelled out in horror, pain and shock, as the Dead continued to rush into him, pushing and wriggling and squeezing. As his body tried to rid itself of them in vain, skin split and tore, opening up the deepest of cuts, until Matthew was little more than a writhing mass of bleeding flesh. It hadn't taken long, but the Dead at last were gone. And no trace of them remained; they were now both of them inside Matthew, who was breathing rapidly and hanging half dead from the ropes and wires that held him high. But he wasn't half dead, thought Lazarus. Nowhere near. This is what Craig had gone through. That thing he'd pulled from him on the shore had been a whole crowd of the Dead that had become one inside him, pushed into him to take back to the land of the Living. Lazarus didn't want to think about what could have happened had they not got to Craig so quickly, if he'd had a chance to escape.

The fallen angel laughed and with the edge of a wing sent a spray of water from a puddle beneath him over Matthew, washing his body clean of blood. Then he grabbed two more of the Dead, and sent them flying towards him. By the time these two had sunk into him, merciful unconsciousness had given him a little reprieve. When it was finally over, Lazarus had counted over thirty Dead now inside Matthew's crowded body.

The fallen angel snapped the ropes and wires holding Matthew to the frame. His body slurped to the ground with a sickening, wet slap, like a drowned man on a mortician's slab. He then heaved the body into the air with one hand, and Matthew just hung there, out cold. The fallen angel looked up at the darkness that covered Simmerdale and raised Matthew above his head with as much effort as Lazarus would need to hold aloft a dead rat.

A shimmer of something flashed through the darkness, and the village shivered, like an earthquake had not just rattled it, but momentarily made everything liquid.

The darkness above the village started to swirl like milk stirred into black coffee, then twist and spiral like smoke caught in a jet stream. It was soon spinning faster and faster, and water was falling from it, heavier than the constant light rain. It looked just like the whirlpool they'd come through, only working up rather than down.

With a triumphant roar, the angel hurled Matthew towards the crazed spinning vortex. He was sucked up into it with not a sound. But the angel wasn't finished. He swept round to the crowd and beckoned to them with a curled finger. From one of the buildings another body was pulled, again strapped to a frame. And this time it wasn't a man. It was a woman.

A single name choked in Lazarus's throat. 'Clair!'

And again Lazarus watched the same process: the Dead yanked from the crowd, thrown into Clair's body. He couldn't tear his eyes away, couldn't block his ears of her screams. He wanted to, but it was impossible. Because Lazarus knew he was responsible for Clair being here in the first place. She'd got involved because of him. And now here she was, living a nightmare beyond all nightmares.

At last, Clair was cast upwards. Then the vortex faded and Simmerdale was cast once again into that thick, soupy darkness.

The Dead drifted back into the houses and shut the doors behind them. The fallen angel stayed for a moment, staring at the Black Shard, tracing its fingers around the carvings Lazarus had seen cut down one side. He remembered it had looked like it had been chipped or smashed or ripped from something much larger. But what? And why was it so important?

The angel let out a howl, then eased itself back into the air on its wings, turned and headed straight for Lazarus and Craig.

Lazarus didn't have time to warn Craig; he threw himself forwards and pulled him to the ground, hand over his mouth. Craig complained, but Lazarus held him tight as the sound of wings flushed overhead and the angel disappeared into the black. Lazarus saw far off in the distance that intense stabbing light again, jabbing out from deep inside the darkness with a laser-like fierceness. The light blinked out. All was quiet.

Lazarus relaxed his grip and rolled off Craig.

'Some warning would've been appreciated,' said Craig, sitting up.

'Wasn't time,' replied Lazarus. 'If we'd been seen, we'd have been completely screwed.'

'Which makes me wonder why we're here at all.'

'I think the Dead have been using this place as a halfway house between the land of the Living and the Dead,' said Lazarus.

'How?'

'The village sits on the edge of two worlds,' explained Lazarus. 'Ours and Hell. Its very presence has caused a weakness in the veil – that whirlpool we used? That's it, I'm sure of it.'

'If it's a weakness, why aren't the Dead just rushing through? What about all that stuff they did to your dad, turning him into the Dark? Wasn't the Dark their weapon to get into the Land of the Living? And what about the Fallen; what have they got to do with this?'

This was something about Craig that Lazarus hadn't missed: the questions.

'Everything's connected,' said Lazarus. 'I don't know how yet, but I'm getting there. The veils between the worlds have failed. And the Fallen are going to use the Dead to wipe us out. To say that they hate humanity is an understatement.'

'Still doesn't explain what they did to me and that Matthew bloke. And Clair.'

Lazarus took a moment to himself, to get his thoughts straight. Some of it still wasn't adding up, but what they'd just seen had got him thinking.

'That commune we drove through, right? The one with the pier we raced off?'

Craig nodded. 'How will I ever forget?'

'It's a cover for the Dead. They've set the place up as a religious retreat, maybe by sending some of the Dead through first to possess a few of the living, some of the locals maybe, I don't know. I think that's what Abaddon's daughter was used for.'

'Nice and out of the way too,' added Craig. 'Less likely to draw a crowd.'

Lazarus nodded; Craig was catching on quick. 'If I'm right, then what I think they're doing is using those who turn up at the commune to bring the Dead back. They probably get people here under the impression they're going to get some spiritual healing, only instead of a bit of yoga, some vegetarian food and a bit of chanting, they find themselves tossed off the end of the pier and filled with the Dead like some kind of sick, twisted taxi service!'

'Then they're sent back up, leave the commune and are out in society.'

Lazarus remembered what Willie had said about the city bloke who'd set up the festival after a visit to the commune; the festival was a part of the plan, too, wasn't it?

'And if Matthew and Clair are anything to go by,' said Lazarus, 'they're each carrying at least thirty of the Dead inside them, so that's one hell of a lot of evil carried by someone who looks like you or me.'

'What now?'

Lazarus glanced back into the darkness to where the fallen angel had gone, then back up through Simmerdale. The place was quiet again, all but for the endless sound of water dripping and seeping and sploshing from every nook and cranny.

'We go after the Black Shard.'

'But isn't it being carried by that fallen angel? And didn't you say we wouldn't stand a chance against it?'

'Yes it is, and yes I did,' said Lazarus. 'You in?'

'Not like I've somewhere else to go, is it?' muttered Craig. 'But I do have a question: how, in the name of all things wrong and twisted and freaky, are we supposed to catch up with it? You did notice its wings, right?'

Lazarus said nothing. Just reached into his pockets and pulled out the keys to the Defender.

22

SLICED, SKEWERED, DECAPITATED

Lazarus and Craig were halfway back through the village when they both realised that the 'We'll just walk through like we belong here, it'll be fine' plan was about to turn into a car crash.

'I see dead people . . .' Craig said.

Lazarus wanted to laugh but he couldn't. It made him wonder if he'd ever laugh again. Life just didn't seem funny any more.

Doors creaked open, swinging out a slew of murky water and grime. The village was closing in on them, like the houses were slipping forward, their doors like drooling mouths, their shuttered windows the drunken eyes of an escaped murderer. If there was ever a bad place to be, this was it; trapped somewhere that was itself imprisoned between Hell and the real, living, breathing, warm world. And he'd got into this because he'd had no choice. His dad had needed him, and despite hardly knowing the bloke, he'd found himself swept along into his secret nightmare.

'Laz . . .'

Craig's voice switched from funny-in-the-face-of-terror to full-on scared.

'I know,' he said. 'They're surrounding us.'

Sometimes, stating the obvious made the situation easier to deal with. This was not one of those sometimes. All it did was make the Defender, their only means of escape, seem even further away.

A flash of movement from his left side. Lazarus let instinct take its course and, without altering his direction, swung his spike round hard, felt it connect, sink in, heard a gurgling scream. He shook free whatever it was he'd just skewered, heard it drop to the ground with a splash.

'That was just to test us,' he said. 'You ready for this?'

Craig said, 'No,' but Lazarus saw him grip Abaddon's scythes. He was taken back then, to a moment that seemed an age ago, but had only been a few days. They'd been at his house, heard a crash in his dad's study, gone through to investigate. Craig had had his back then and he had it now, no question. It was some consolation. Not much, but it was enough to light a flame inside Lazarus that burned white hot.

He stopped. The Dead did the same.

'Mate, what are we doing?'

No reply. Lazarus was looking around now, taking it all in, the village, the Dead, the darkness hiding in the alleyways between some of the houses. And a thought struck him: he was as much a part of this world now as the one he'd grown up in. He wasn't just a Keeper, he was something more.

He'd died twice, fought off demons, battled with his own twisted mother, seen and done things too horrible to ever be able to come out unscathed. And no way was he going to be afraid now. Not here, not in front of these things. He wouldn't give them the satisfaction.

He snapped round to Craig.

'Do as I do, step where I step, kill anything that comes close, and run like stink, got it?'

'Totally,' Craig nodded. 'Where are we going?'

Lazarus ignored the shake in his friend's voice, snapped back round again and took off left.

A howl swept through the Dead like a Mexican wave. Lazarus felt it like a shockwave but was too focused on what was in front of him, standing between him, and where he was heading.

He hit the first one in the head with such force that the thorns jutting out the back of his hand tore it away at the neck. Momentum ripped it off the thorns and sent it spinning hard into the wall of the building behind it, and it exploded like a watermelon filled with plastic explosive. The second one fell back from him, but tripped, and Lazarus kept running, stomping its face into the dirt with a shocked gurgle that cut short when its skull caved in. Behind him, Craig yelled out, but he didn't have time to stop and check everything was OK, he just had to trust in his friend and in the faint scent of hope.

Having seen two of their own taken down with such speed, the Dead still in front of Lazarus hesitated. That was their biggest, and their last, mistake. Lazarus brought his spike round in a deadly arc, cutting the first one in half, before his weapon lodged against the spine of the next one along. As he went to dislodge it, a glint of metal slashed past and he saw Craig dive in front and finish off what he'd started. Abaddon's scythes were clearly more than capable of dealing with the Dead, even in the hands of Craig.

Craig glanced at Lazarus, sweat beading on his neck. 'We're heading somewhere, right? You've got a plan?'

Lazarus nodded into the gloom between the two houses directly in front of them. 'It'll be too narrow for them to swamp us,' he said. 'If we're quick, we can get through and out the other side before they realise what we're doing. Right?'

Craig didn't need telling twice and bounded ahead. This time it was Lazarus who was taking up the rear and he did so with surgical-like efficiency, despatching the Dead like he was doing them a favour. Each one he stamped on, cut, sliced, skewered, decapitated, ripped apart, eviscerated, was one less to threaten someone innocent and alive.

Craig was in the alleyway now. Two of the Dead had managed to get between him and Lazarus, but they hadn't lasted long against the scythes. Lazarus jumped over their rotting carcasses and was with his friend again.

'How far to the other side?'

'Just a few metres,' said Craig, breathing hard. 'The way's still clear.'

'Won't be for long,' said Lazarus, wiping gore from his face. 'Look, they're moving already! They'll be round to block us off any moment! Leg it!'

Craig sprang forward like someone had set him on fire, and Lazarus was close behind. He'd never been able to run as fast as Craig, despite being generally the fitter of the two. Craig had always had this unnatural speed when it came to sprinting. Lazarus had seen him use it to piss off more than a few of the sportier lads at school during PE.

The end of the alley shot past and Lazarus and Craig were out the other side. In front of them, the rear gardens of the houses were ripped in half, dropping down to the dark plain below. And somewhere on that plain was the Defender. But where?

'Which way now?'

Lazarus got his bearings, remembered and pointed

right. 'That's the way we came in. Back the other way and we'll be at the cemetery again.'

A thick, deep moan bowled out ahead of them and Lazarus saw the Dead start to spill out in front of them. If they didn't move now, they'd be trapped.

Without a word, Lazarus and Craig dug deep and exploded forwards.

The Dead howled and scratched and stretched and clawed, but no matter what they did, they couldn't bring the two boys down. Those that got close lost limbs, had their guts ripped out, were smashed down and crushed in the rush.

The carved stone sign for Simmerdale zipped past. The way ahead was clear. Lazarus's legs were burning now, lactic acid was building. He was gasping for air, running on reserves he didn't even know that he had. At his side, Craig was no better off, but he wasn't quitting either.

They charged from the village, down the final stretch of the ruined road, and half stumbled, half fell on to the plain. Ahead in the dark, Lazarus made out the solid, square shape of the Defender. That was the finish line and with renewed effort he pushed on. Not far now, not far . . .

Craig yelped and dropped to the ground. But if Lazarus stopped now, if he hesitated for one second, the Dead would have them. He couldn't lift Craig; if he tried to carry him, he'd be slowed down. They'd both be finished. His only choice was to leave him and get to the Defender.

Craig's cries of pain and terror raked iron claws across Lazarus's skin, but he ignored them as the Defender appeared out of the dark. Unable to slow down, he slammed into the grille. It winded him, but he kept moving, crawling his way round the wing and in through the driver's door. He fired up the engine, hit the lights. Ahead, all he could see was every zombie-movie lover's wet dream; a great fat wash of the Dead swarming towards him, and between him and them lay his terrified friend.

Lazarus crashed the truck into first, released the handbrake and accelerated. The Defender leapt forwards like it was hungry, the tyres digging into the ground, chewing it up and spewing it out the back.

The Dead were close, so much so that Lazarus could

see their howling rage pulling their faces into agonising, bare-toothed grimaces. Craig was in their sights and they were going to pile into him and rip him to pieces and enjoy every last breath he had and . . .

But Lazarus wasn't going to let that happen. Eyes narrowed, he drove to the right of Craig and took a wide sweep at the Dead, blocking them from getting to his friend. They were too surprised by his attack to do anything about it except stare in bewildered shock as he piled through them like shop-window dummies. They bounced off the bonnet, were sent spinning left and right, broken and smashed and disappeared under the wheels with black screams and gurgling crunches of mashed flesh and bone.

Lazarus brought the Defender back round to Craig. He may have bought them some time, but not much; the Dead were ignoring their wounded and, with renewed anger, were back on them, picking up speed.

Lazarus jumped out, was at Craig's side.

'I thought you were bloody well leaving me behind!' said Craig as Lazarus helped him to his feet, pulled open the passenger door.

'No chance!' shouted Lazarus. 'Now, stop with the

wounded soldier stuff and get in!'

Craig had little choice as Lazarus heaved him up into his seat and leaned over to strap him in.

Lazarus was back in the driver's seat just as an advanced party of the Dead threw themselves against the Defender, pulling themselves up on to it, crawling on to the bonnet, like monkeys at a safari park.

'Ready?' asked Lazarus.

Craig was incredulous. 'You mean it's going to get worse than this?'

'Only one way to find out.'

23
GIANT MAGGOTS

Lazarus glared through the windscreen. Two of the Dead were pulling at the windscreen wipers, punching the glass, their hands coming apart with the force of it. Behind them, the rest of the Dead were spilling forwards, rolling over each other in their lustful urgency to get to Lazarus and Craig.

Lazarus gunned it.

The Dead exploded in a gut-churning carousel of spurting blood and splintered bone as Lazarus rammed the Defender into them with all the tact of a bulldozer doing ninety. He wasn't about to slam on the brakes.

A combination of speed and weight made the truck unstoppable, but still some of the Dead had a go, launching themselves at it only to be shredded by the very thing they were trying to halt. It was like watching rag dolls being thrown at a high-speed train.

A grim grin slipped across Lazarus's face as the windscreen bloodied up and the damaged wiper did its best to clear the hideous smears. It didn't do a very good job, but he could still see just enough to keep the Defender aiming in the right direction, taking it right towards Simmerdale.

'We're going back?' said Craig. 'But I thought we were after that fallen angel?'

'Don't want to skirt round it and waste any more time,' Lazarus replied, dropping from fourth to third as the last of the Dead fell by the wayside and the village came up directly ahead. 'We don't know what lies to each side of the village, we don't want to get lost. But we do know our way through. Quicker and safer.'

'I'll ignore the word safer,' said Craig.

The Defender raced from the plain and up on to the road leading through the village. When they arrived in the single main street, it was clear, silent. But in a bad way, thought Lazarus, like the village was closing in on them, melting and slipping into a pile of rubble and ruin that would have them trapped.

Craig shook Lazarus by the shoulder.

'Hey, why are you slowing down? What's wrong?'

Lazarus shook his head, squeezed his eyes back into focus.

'Sorry,' he said, 'but this place . . . I can feel it crushing down on me. I can't explain it. I've got used to the nausea now that I'm here. But it's like the place can smell me or something; it knows I'm here!'

'Then let's just get the hell out and fast!' yelled Craig. 'Move it, Laz!'

Lazarus didn't reply. He couldn't. Something was now happening up ahead of them and it had his full attention.

Craig followed Laz's wild-eyed stare.

'What the . . .'

The road in the centre of the village was rising and crumbling and falling away; something was pushing up from beneath it. What Lazarus thought at first was water gushing out through the widening cracks, he soon realised was blood, thick and red and oozing and steaming. The ground continued to rise and soon the mound in front of them was blocking the street completely. Then, through the broken, bloodied earth, something started to push its way through, filling the air with the sound of people being crushed in an earthquake. Whatever it was, Lazarus couldn't make out and didn't want to. It looked like a huge pile of giant maggots, twisting and churning into each other. But the true horror of what it was only became apparent when two enormous arms burst through the ground and started to heave the thing up and out of the hole now cutting off their escape.

They weren't giant maggots. They were limbs. Arms, legs, torsos, screaming agonised heads; the monster was made up from a thousand broken bodies, all twisting into each other, to become a giant formed of hideous flesh.

It reached out and used one of the houses to gain more purchase. Then continued to heave itself out. Its head, if it could be called that, turned to the Defender and a great black hole opened in its centre. A howl raged out on a slurry of body parts that rained down on the Defender. Inside the truck, Lazarus and Craig were almost deafened by the torrent of gore as it slammed down on to the roof, the bonnet, bouncing off and down to the ground, covering everything in a spew of black, rotten meat.

'That alleyway,' Lazarus nodded to the left. 'Reckon we'll fit?'

He slipped the gearstick into first, stamped on the accelerator, and yanked the steering wheel round as hard and fast as he could.

The Defender's rear end spun out. The monster roared and let out a fresh barrage of hellish vomit, but Lazarus refused to be distracted; the alleyway was in his sights. And he wasn't about to let it end here. No way. Everyone was counting on him. And his dad.

The entrance to the alleyway shot up to meet them fast. Lazarus squeezed his own shoulders in, as if making himself thinner would help at all.

Amazingly, he judged it right, and the Defender tore out of the main street and into the alleyway. But it was only just wide enough and the wing mirrors were smashed off by the walls.

A thunderous sound rumbled from behind them and Craig looked back to see the monster ripping apart the houses to chase after them.

Flying out of the alleyway, Lazarus pulled right and just kept on going. In front of them now were the ruined gardens and backyards of the houses, nothing but muddied mounds and piles of black earth.

Lazarus didn't have time to wonder if driving over it would smash the truck to pieces. They had no choice. Either they raced out this way, or they waited for whatever that thing was to crush them to a pulp.

He didn't look back. But then he didn't need to; Craig had his eyes on the thing, as it came crashing out of the alleyway, bringing the houses down on either side of it like they were made of no more than a child's toy building blocks.

'You need to shift it,' said Craig, not exactly helpfully.

'What the hell do you think I'm trying to do?' Laz snarled back. 'It's not like we're out for a Sunday drive, you idiot!'

Something landed on the roof of the Defender with such a clang that Lazarus was surprised whatever it was hadn't just crashed right through.

'What was that?'

'You don't want to know.'

Another clang, just as loud.

'Is it throwing stuff at us?'

'You could say that,' said Craig.

Lazarus was about to punch Craig on the arm to get him to be more specific when his window was smashed in and something grabbed for him. He turned to see shredded flesh hanging off the carcass of a woman who looked as if she'd had a fight with a tank. Her face was flat, the features all pushed together and twisted into a snarl. Her chest was crushed in and her arms looked like they'd been through a meat grinder.

Lazarus yelled out, tried to shake the dead woman's hand off him, but it was impossible if he was to keep the Defender heading in the right direction.

'Craig! Do something!'

The woman was pulling herself in through the window now, snapping her broken jaws at Lazarus's face like she was trying to French kiss him. And her breath was of raw sewage.

Craig unclipped his seatbelt so that he could punch the woman hard enough to knock her back out through the window. But she was still hanging on.

'Lean back!'

Lazarus obeyed and saw the blade of one of Abaddon's

scythes flick past his face to cut through the woman's fingers. She disappeared with a yell, and went straight under the Defender's rear wheels, which crushed her to an oily slick along the ground.

But there was no time for celebration as, from the back of the Defender, something slammed its way in through the rear-door window, landing on the floor. It was on its feet before either Lazarus or Craig could react, and dragged Craig into the back.

Lazarus was helpless. He couldn't stop driving so couldn't help Craig. He just had to hope his best mate had it in him to deal with what had snatched him. All he could do now was focus on his driving, and do it as hard and fast as he could and get away from the monstrous thing tearing up the ground behind them as it made chase, ripping bodies from its limbs and throwing them screaming and tumbling through the air like fleshy grenades to try and stop them.

The inside of the vehicle exploded with the sound of the fight behind him. Lazarus was able to snatch glances at it in his driver's window, but he couldn't tell who was winning, if either of them were.

A scythe cut through the air and the creature yelled out.

'Kill it, Craig! Rip that bastard thing apart! Do it!'

The fight grew louder still, until with a sickening, gut-churning crunch, it fell quiet.

A bloody hand landed on Lazarus's shoulder and he nearly leapt out of his seat.

'That's something I don't want to do again in a hurry,' said Craig, as Lazarus saw his mate pull himself back into the front of the Defender and buckle up. He was a mess, but Lazarus figured most of the blood belonged to what was now lying broken in the back of the Defender and slowly rotting away and dissolving.

'You can tell me all about it later,' said Lazarus. 'I think it's about time we got out of here, agreed?'

Craig didn't nod. He just let his head fall back against his headrest.

Lazarus saw the cemetery coming up ahead. All he had to do now was swing right as he came up to it, pull them back on to the road leading out of Simmerdale, and then hope to God that they'd lose the monster in the darkness that stretched out in front of them.

A body flew overhead, landed in front of them. Lazarus didn't give it a chance to get up, driving straight into it, bursting it like a water balloon. Another came, then another, and soon they were falling all round them like rain, bursting as they landed like bags filled with the ruined mess of a fatal car accident.

It knows we're getting away! Lazarus realised.

With renewed fervour, he focused on what he was doing, ignored the howls and screams and thumps and crunches as the Defender made quick work of the Dead unlucky enough to land in their way.

At the cemetery, Lazarus dropped down a gear, heaved the truck right, saw the road, bounced them out on to it, pulled left again, and accelerated hard. The engine screamed like it was a part of him, the pistons firing up his determination to get them out of this and to his dad.

He brought the Defender out of Simmerdale and back out on to the black plain. In the driver's mirror he could see more of the Dead being flung at them, but they were falling short now, landing like sad puppets, broken and busted. He could just make out that distant light he'd seen before, the one the fallen angel had flown towards.

He didn't allow himself to question what the light was – just drove straight for it . . .

24

HIDDEN HORROR

The bright white beams from the headlamps shot out from the front of the Defender to burn a tunnel through the dark ahead. Lazarus stared into it, still focused on the light, which was growing longer, like it was gradually sweeping round to meet them, the beam of a searchlight creeping through the gloom. But it gave away no clue as to where they were heading, or what they might find when they got there. They were just driving. And around them, the darkness stood like it was watching them pass through it, utterly disinterested in their purpose.

'If it's all the same with you,' said Craig, 'I'd prefer it if we never went to Simmerdale ever again.'

'Gets my vote,' replied Lazarus. 'You holding up OK?'

'After everything that's happened, I don't think I'll ever

be fully OK again, know what I mean?'

Totally, thought Lazarus.

'Whatever that thing was,' said Craig, 'it didn't exactly like us, did it?'

'We don't belong here,' said Lazarus. 'Being as we're not actually dead.'

Though, as those words slipped from his mouth, Lazarus wasn't quite so sure how true they were. He'd already died twice. And then he remembered something that had been said to him by Red, about how death was in him now. It seemed that for better or worse he now had a foot on both sides, in the land of the Living, and in the land of the Dead.

Craig shook his head. 'That's not my point. What I'm saying is that, like the Dead, it didn't just turn up or go after you by accident. It knew you were there! Sensed you or something. The Dead were too occupied by what was happening to that Matthew bloke to do anything when we were hiding in the cemetery, but after that? When we walked through their town? They came at us all at once.'

Lazarus didn't want to think about what Craig had

said, but it made sense. He was the Keeper after all. And he had a feeling now that not just all of the Dead, but Hell itself, knew about him. It wasn't the kind of thought that sat well in his stomach. Particularly with where they were now, and where they were heading.

For a while, neither spoke, instead just stared ahead into the void they were sliding through, the only sound that of the thrum of the Defender's engine and the drone of the tyres on the ground.

'That Matthew bloke.' Craig broke the silence, shuffling on his seat, putting a foot up on the dashboard. 'Where's he belong in all this?'

Lazarus thought back to when he'd first seen Matthew, how insane he'd seemed, running out in front of them and heavy on the doom and gloom. Whatever crazy crap he'd been talking, Abaddon had taken some of it seriously. And, like Craig had said, he'd found the whirlpool.

'Matthew was at the lake when we arrived,' Lazarus began, actually quite thankful for something to talk about. It would at least take his mind off the endless darkness slipping by outside, and also what his overactive imagination was telling him might lie beyond it. 'He was crazy, and I mean lock-em-up-and-throw-away-the-key nutjob.'

'Serious?'

Lazarus laughed, couldn't help himself. 'Just after Arielle parked up, he ran out in front of us, half naked and wearing a placard over his chest with something on it about the lake being dangerous!'

'Piss off!'

Lazarus shook his head. 'Like I said: crazy.'

'You said he found the whirlpool, but I don't see how that was difficult considering it was large enough to swallow us in this thing.'

Lazarus remembered everything Matthew had told him, everything he'd shown him. He may have been crazy, but it was the kind of crazy that came with a huge amount of intelligence; Matthew knew he'd stumbled on something big and his madness probably stemmed from losing his daughter, his marriage and his career as much as anything else.

'He found the whirlpool by accident,' explained Lazarus, and told Craig how Matthew had first come to the lake because of his daughter. 'His hobby was diving, so, as the commune was by a lake, he brought his kit with him to keep himself occupied, I guess.'

'Diving alone?'

Lazarus nodded. 'There's a legend attached to the lake, right? About how it wasn't always there, that this village sat where the lake now is.'

'Creepy.'

'But it's no legend,' said Lazarus. 'The story's true. It was Abaddon's village; Simmerdale.'

'You mean the place we've just been through actually used to be somewhere else? On Earth?'

'Look,' said Lazarus, trying not to let his voice betray just how tired he was feeling, 'I can't be arsed to go into it all now, but all you need to know is that Abaddon cursed the village and sent it to Hell. The lake covered it up, kind of erased it from existence I guess.'

'And Matthew went to look for it.'

'He didn't find it,' said Lazarus. 'It's probably a bit like looking for the Loch Ness monster. But what he did find was something else.'

'The whirlpool?'

Lazarus shook his head. 'Not at first, no. What he

actually found first of all was that where the bottom of the lake was, well, it wasn't.'

'That's gibberish. The bottom of the lake wasn't what?'

'It wasn't there!' said Lazarus. 'And of all the people you'd expect to not take it seriously, Abaddon actually did.'

'Abaddon? Really?'

'When I told him what Matthew had said, about how the lake had got deeper, but he didn't know how deep, and all this other really nuts stuff about really high carbon dioxide concentration in the water and the lake exploding, he went and walked out into the lake and came back with you.'

'And Matthew said all that?'

'Like I said,' yawned Lazarus, rubbing his weary eyes. 'Crazy.'

Craig swept condensation from the passenger-door window and stared out into utter nothingness. 'Not really,' he said. 'The CO_2 in the lake could explode in a massive gas bubble if there was a seismic disturbance or something. But I don't see how that could happen; it's not like this place sits on a tectonically active area, is it?'

Lazarus had to really work at not letting his jaw drop into the footwell. How on earth did Craig know anything about what Matthew had been talking about?

'You sound like one of those rubbish programmes on National Geographic.'

'That would be because I watch National Geographic,' Craig replied and looked over at Lazarus with a somewhat superior air. 'It's very educational.'

Lazarus laughed. 'You do talk some crap, you know that, don't you?'

'I'm serious!' said Craig. 'Matthew may have been mad, but the exploding lake thing is for real. It's called a limnic eruption. Happened in . . . er . . .'

Craig paused, then stared up at the roof of the Defender as though that was where he would find what he was trying to say.

Lazarus was about to repeat the name of the lake Matthew had spoken of when Craig's face lit up and he said, 'Lake Nyos! That was it! This place in Africa. Couple of thousand people died, I think. Really freaky if you ask me. And Matthew thought that could happen at the lake? Seriously?'

Lazarus couldn't believe it. Flexing his hands to stop them seizing up on the steering wheel, he said, 'You know more about it than I do. That's the place Matthew was talking about.'

'Not worth worrying about though,' said Craig. 'Even if there was enough CO_2 in the bottom of the lake to cause an eruption, it would need something to cause it to burst upwards. And short of dropping a shedload of explosives into it, it just ain't going to happen.'

'True,' said Lazarus.

Craig hadn't finished. 'The only reason so many people died at Nyos was because the gas rolled over all the nearby villages. I haven't seen much of where the lake is, but it didn't exactly look like a populated area. The gas could burst out and no one would ever know.'

When Craig stopped talking, Lazarus was struck by everything at once; what Matthew had said, the village, the Dead already slipping through, the bloke Willie had spoken of who'd set up the festival, the Fallen.

Everything slotted into place with awful precision.

'You've gone white,' said Craig. 'Well, when I say white, I mean you were pretty white already, so whatever colour *that* is I don't know. Transparent? Is that a colour? You look ill.'

'The festival!' gasped Lazarus.

'What festival?'

Lazarus jammed on the brakes and the Defender skidded to a halt, forcing him and Craig to lunge forward and strain against their seatbelts. He was playing back images in his head, the thousands he'd seen crowding into the fields around the lake. The tents going up. The stages. The music. All of those people, utterly unaware of the horror hidden beneath the lake . . .

Craig coughed. 'What the hell did you do that for?'

'I know what's going to happen,' said Lazarus. 'And if it does, we're in the shit.'

25
HELL

Craig emptied the last drop of petrol from the fuel can and placed it back into its cage, attached to the rear of the Defender. The gloopy darkness had now turned into a sludgy grey, and the light was closer still.

'We need to shift,' he said. 'There's something about the light – or lack of it – I don't like. Feels like it could just reach out and snatch us away at any minute. And why does everywhere smell scorched like a fire that's been dead for a few days?'

Lazarus said nothing and strapped the fuel can in with some ragged webbing hanging from its cage. He didn't have answers to the questions, but knew that those answers lay not too far away now.

They both ran quickly back round the Defender and jumped in, slamming the doors behind them.

Lazarus figured that the thin aluminium shell of the truck would give about as much protection against what could attack them here, as a duvet would against an intruder armed with an axe. But it was still good to be back inside.

The strange white light looked larger now, thought Lazarus. And it was clearly moving, coming at them from their right, but so slowly it was like trying to watch the hour hand on a clock move round; somehow it swept from number to number, but actually seeing it move was next to impossible. But Lazarus still didn't know what it was, why the fallen angel had headed towards it, or how far they still had to go to get there. He felt like he'd been driving for years.

So when they burst without warning into a place of blinding light, it was no surprise that Lazarus nearly lost control, and spun the truck.

Craig swore. Lazarus, trying to regain control of the vehicle, saw him cover his eyes with his hands, as the light from outside burned away the darkness they'd almost grown used to. The spin seemed to just keep going, like they were suddenly on sheet ice. The tyres couldn't grip, spun uselessly. All Lazarus could do was hold on and wait for it all to stop. He closed his eyes.

Silence.

Head still spinning, despite the Defender having come to a standstill, Lazarus kept his eyes closed. He was leaning forward against the steering wheel, his head between his hands. He could hear his own breathing, Craig's too, and the vehicle itself creaking and groaning. His ears were ringing, a thin whining sound trying to pierce his brain. He squeezed his eyes to get rid of it, gripped the steering wheel hard, wished he was somewhere else, because that always worked, didn't it?

Lazarus didn't want to open his eyes. Whatever was out there in that light he just didn't want to see it. And the sensation was a little unexpected. Not the fear itself, but that it was a fear of the light instead of the dark. That something bad could be so bright seemed in itself a juxtaposition. Evil was darkness, good was the light. Right? *Right?*

Wrong . . .

Lazarus opened his eyes . . .

. . . to Hell.

And it rushed in all at once, exploding inside his head with the intensity of a star going super nova. The force of it was like he'd been thrust into a wind tunnel, and he slammed back in his seat. A shiver hacked at him and his skin felt like it was being whipped and pulled by fishhooks.

Above them, the sky was a bubbling, boiling thing of grey cloud, rolling and folding in and on to itself. It looked more like liquid that could in a moment just burst and drown the land below it, land stretched out in all directions, flat and endless.

Lazarus glanced into the driver's mirror, expecting to see reflected in it the darkness they had just come from. But he saw nothing. Just more of this endless plain under that awful, boiling sky. Wherever they'd come from had disappeared. Turning back was no longer an option.

Craig just sat there, shoulders slumped, face emotionless, like every expression he could ever muster had been burned away by what lay in front of them.

Under the sky, the flat, bright plain jarred with everything Lazarus knew and understood. It was both a thing of the most astonishing beauty, unlike anywhere he had ever seen or could imagine, and also somewhere of such awful horror, it was all he could do to hold on to his sanity and not lose it completely right there, and go all out with the crazy.

The landscape was a sweep of the most lush, swaying grass Lazarus had ever seen. It made him think of the kind of place David Attenborough would go all breathy for in a voiceover; a savannah unlike anything on Earth. A faint wind gave the grass a sea-like quality and in all directions islands of soft hills and forests could be seen. It was a place of fierce beauty, the reality behind the imagining of Heaven. Yet something wasn't right. Something so completely and utterly wrong that it resonated with a jarring discord that, despite there being no actual sound, Lazarus wanted to crush his hands against his ears to block it out.

The thing, the hideous, terrifying yell of terror, which scratched and bit and crushed every sense of beauty this landscape offered, stood at its very centre. And it did so with such a sense of awful purpose that it seemed to Lazarus that they, and everything around them, were being sucked into it like water down a drain, galaxies into a black hole.

Lazarus remembered again Abaddon's words, only this time it was as though the dead priest was right next to him, breathing across him with his rotten, vinegary stench: 'The village is in Hell, Lazarus. But it lies in the distant, endless black lands which surround it, and out of reach of the terrible, burning reality of that place.'

Here, in front of them, was the truth behind those words: the terrible, burning reality.

Bursting out of the ground like a great black tooth to pierce the sky, stood a tower that defied all logic.

It was miles wide, it had to be. Lazarus wasn't sure how far away it actually was, but its immensity was without question. It was like it had its own gravitational pull. Trying to stare up it and spy its hidden peak made him dizzy, like it would come toppling down on him. Around its base, the ground rose up in great mountainous rifts, each so high the tops were crusted with what Lazarus guessed were ice and snow. The tower itself was of a substance so black it seemed to cancel out all light; not a reflection stood out on its surface, like any bright thing that attempted to scale it would be swallowed whole. Through a valley carved into the rocky rifts at its base, Lazarus saw what he could only assume to be the tower's entrance. It was like looking into the mouth of a shark, the edges of it like row upon row of teeth just waiting for you to enter so they could tear you apart, feed on you. And the tower, Lazarus thought, looked starving.

But the tower wasn't the worst of it. It was the light that it cast, the light they had followed from Simmerdale to here. And what it did.

Blindingly bright, it cut through the landscape, from the base of the tower to the horizon, like a great sabre. And it burned in an instant everything it touched to dust and ash. Lazarus could see far-off billowing clouds of smoke, boiling with raging torrents of flame, which, though miles away, were advancing. Nothing could escape it and nothing did. The only way to do so would be to keep ahead of it. For ever. And even more impossibly, Lazarus could see that the land the bright beam of light had devastated was slowly rejuvenating, growing lush again. It was as though Heaven had been created here, but only as an eternal reminder of what could have been; everything about it being in a constant state of destruction and creation. An endless repetition of blinding beauty and agonising hideousness, as the beauty burned away. To be trapped here, Lazarus knew then, would be unimaginable. But then, surely, that was the point . . .

A hollow, terrified cry croaked from his throat. He wanted to get away, forget he'd ever been here, run as quickly and as far away as possible, and never look back. Ever. But then this was the kind of place you could never truly run from. It would always be there, a black hole burned into your soul.

Lazarus rubbed his eyes, partly to push away tears, partly to help gather himself and remind him why he was there. But the reasons seemed distant now, like wisps of mist being burned off in the morning sun, and he had to fight to find them, make sense of them: his father . . . the Black Shard . . . What was all this about?

'Laz?'

Craig's voice made Lazarus visibly jump. He saw his own vivid fright scratched into the face of his friend.

'Whatever we're here to do,' said Craig, 'Let's get it done and get the hell away as fast as we can.'

Lazarus nodded, but now, in the presence of the tower, he had no idea what he was here to do at all. He was hopeless, weak, crushed.

Craig pointed through the windscreen.

'You see those?'

Lazarus squinted to see what Craig was pointing at. He couldn't make anything out, his brain so rammed with the horror of the tower to see anything else.

'What?'

'Something's moving round the tower. Like vultures circling something dead on the ground. But it's not vultures, is it, Laz?'

Lazarus saw then what Craig was talking about. Up the whole height of the tower, from the ground and up into the clouds, great winged things were swooping around it. They were like vultures, thought Lazarus, but he knew they were anything but.

'Fallen angels,' said Craig. 'Right?'

Lazarus kept staring. He'd noticed something else about them. It was as though they were flying to the point of exhaustion, trying to stay ahead of the burning light of the tower. He could see some of them peeling off from the rest to tumble to the ground, crashing into others. Some slowed, the light caught them, and they lit up like a firework.

Craig said, 'We have to go there, don't we?'

Lazarus knew he didn't need to answer. This time it was Craig's turn with the rhetorical.

Silently, slowly, but with a grim determination to finish this, Lazarus slipped the gearstick into first, aimed the bonnet for the tower, and hammered the accelerator into the floor.

26
RED

'You hear that?'

Lazarus had phased out everything but the tower.

'Hear what?'

'That weird sizzling sound, like bacon spitting under a grill. Which reminds me, I'm getting hungry.'

Lazarus tried to focus on what Craig had just said. But the tower, the great black monstrosity, blocked everything else out, like someone had pressed a mute button on his whole life. Then he noticed the sound. At first he heard nothing more than the Defender eating its way through the tall grass that stretched out in front of it. But then another sound became apparent. It was faint at first, distant like the buzz of electricity racing through an overhead pylon. But the more he focused on it, the clearer it became.

'You hearing it now?'

'Just,' said Lazarus.

Craig shrugged. 'I think it's one of those sounds that's just always there in the background, you know? It's like you only really notice it once it's not there any more.'

'Like when there's a power cut and the house falls really quiet?'

'Exactly,' nodded Craig. 'But I still don't know what it is.'

But Lazarus did. As soon as he'd heard it, he'd found himself drawn towards the only thing in this place that it could be.

He pointed out through the window. 'It's that,' he said, and watched Craig's eyes move towards what he was pointing at, then widen in disbelief. That such an emotion was possible in a place like this was testament to how awful it was. 'And the reason we can hear it is because it's getting too bloody close!'

The sound was the bright light blasting out of the tower to scorch the ground and everything else in its path. Flames ripped the earth into a torrent of liquid, bubbling heat, smoke and ash. It was like staring into the mouth of an erupting volcano. And Lazarus somehow knew the light had suddenly sensed them and was not only seeking them out, but had sped up to catch them.

Lazarus heard Craig say his name, but then his voice was cut off with a choke.

'Don't worry,' he turned to his friend, heaving a look of almost-confidence on to his face. 'We'll make it!'

But the Defender was going flat out; it had nothing left to give. Too much luck was playing out in this and Lazarus didn't like it.

Ahead, the swaying grass was growing thinner the closer they drew to the tower. The wheels were kicking dust up in great asthmatic clouds, so thick that it vanished the way they had come from view, as if it had never existed.

Lazarus's hands were slick with sweat against the steering wheel like the stuff was just gushing from the pores in his skin. And it wasn't just from the stress of the moment, but the heat of the ground burning under the light. It brought with it the realisation that the light didn't need to reach them to turn them to ash; the heat radiating from it was so intense, there was every chance it would do it in the next few minutes.

The beam of light was close. The flames rose so high into the sky, that Lazarus could no longer see their top. It was like racing against a giant forest of fire, the flames like vast leaves fluttering in the heat, burning up into the sky to be replaced by ferocious new growth.

Lazarus forced himself to turn from the furnace and focus on the tower, when something slammed into the Defender with such force that the back end swung round to point it in the opposite direction. Lazarus tried to control the spin, but it was no good and he let the Defender just go with it, instead concentrating on not letting his head slam against the window when the truck finally came to a halt. It didn't work, and his skull ricocheted off the glass with a dull thud, forcing his eyes shut with the stab of pain.

For a second or two, Lazarus was dizzy, and opening his eyes, the world spun round him. Gripping the steering wheel, he squeezed his eyes shut to pull himself out of it.

'What the hell was that?' yelled Craig.

Lazarus made no reply. Instead, he went to pull the

truck round to point again at the tower, when something not only rammed into it again, but settled on the roof with such a weight that the windscreen popped out, and what was left of the door windows shattered like ice.

Lazarus and Craig ducked, both expecting the roof to cave in and crush them like a tomato under a steamroller. But the roof held. Footprints sunk into it like they were melting the metal around them. They then walked from the rear of the truck to directly over their heads, the footprints perfect like imprints in the sand.

Lazarus saw Craig look at the advancing footprints and then across at him; he didn't need to voice the question scratched into the look of terror now in his eyes.

With a nod at his friend, he had another go at getting the Defender moving, but as he put his foot on the accelerator, the wheels spun. He tried again, but the same thing happened. They were stuck!

'What the hell's wrong?' asked Craig, his voice raked with fear. He was drenched in sweat, the heat from the flames close to torching them both to a cinder.

Lazarus tried again. Nothing.

'We're stuck!'

'We can't be!'

'Well, we bloody well are!'

They had to shout to be heard above the now deafening sound of the flames.

'Try again!'

'What the hell do you think I'm doing?'

Craig went to say something else, but a jolt of movement pitched the Defender and the ground in front of it disappeared. Lazarus felt his stomach sink as something lifted them off the ground.

'Lazarus . . .' said Craig.

'I know!' Lazarus snapped back. 'But there's nothing I can do about it, is there?'

'But we're flying!'

Lazarus looked outside to see the ground rushing past as they accelerated quickly towards the tower. What on earth was doing this to them? He had no doubt it was the thing that had landed on their roof. He was also pretty sure he didn't want to find out what it was.

Lazarus could only guess at what speed they were doing. The ground below was a blur, and the tower was approaching so fast his only thought was that if they hit it at this speed there would be nothing left.

The flames were too close now. Some were even licking through the air in front of them, the Defender blasting through regardless. The windscreen wipers were on fire. The paintwork was bubbling and peeling off. And the acrid smell of the tyres melting was catching in his throat.

No way were they going to make it. No way in Hell.

But just as Lazarus was sure his last moments were going to be spent going up in flames like a firework, the ground came up fast and the Defender, caught in the momentum, bounced and spun forwards like a fairground ride gone crazy. And the world outside slipped into a blur of colours and flame and smoke and darkness.

Lazarus was shaking. He was cold, and he shivered in his sweat-drenched clothes, despite the obvious heat of where they now were. He could make out little of the place, but he had no doubt that they were inside the tower. To his left, Craig was snoring. He must've fallen unconscious in the fierceness of the spin. Lazarus reached out to shake him awake, but something stopped him.

Blinking, he glared through the Defender's glass-less windscreen to see a tall figure approaching. It seemed to pull inwards the darkness that surrounded it, like it was forming itself from it, folding it in and around it as it walked. From its back, great wings splayed outwards, reaching round and forward, almost as though they were trying to encase the Defender.

The figure halted just in front of the bonnet.

'Welcome to Babel, Lazarus . . .'

The sound of that voice burned away any haziness in Lazarus's brain, his vision swept clean, and he recognised who and what it was that had saved them from the flames.

'Red!'

In that moment of recognition, Lazarus saw everything that had happened all at once, his memories ripped from him like film from a reel, clickety-clacking for one last view before the final scene. But Red looked different now. That dark figure, who had appeared in his house stripped of his skin, drenched in blood, decomposing in front of him, was now not just healed, but perfect in every way. Even partially hidden as Red was by the shadows inside the tower, Lazarus could see his beauty, feel it almost, like heat from a flame.

Lazarus climbed out of the Defender, clasping his spike in his hand, the thorns slipping with ease and no pain through his palm, his flesh, and out the other side.

'You look different.'

Red's face broke into a chilled smile of exquisite teeth.

'I feel different,' he replied. 'Better.'

Lazarus didn't like the way Red said those words. Better, he thought, might not necessarily be a good thing.

'You threw yourself into the veil to seal it shut. How come you're here now?'

Lazarus remembered that moment, when after trying to find his own father in the land of the Dead, Red had saved him and Craig by throwing them back through the veil, then used himself to seal it shut.

'I could ask you the same question,' said Red, his voice edgy, as if at any moment it could explode in anger, and he was fighting to keep calm.

Lazarus had seen Red angry; it wasn't something he wanted to see again. Ever.

'Your arrival is a surprise, Lazarus. You are lucky that I sensed you close by and followed my instincts, despite myself. But you should not be here.'

'You know, I keep telling myself the same thing.'

A laugh slipped from Red but disappeared almost immediately, like their surroundings had snuffed it candle-wick dead.

'I mean it!' snarled Red. 'This is no place for you! Why are you here?'

Lazarus heard sharp teeth and claws in Red's words. 'The Black Shard,' he answered. 'Both pieces have been found. The Fallen have taken it. The Dead are massing in Abaddon's village in the black lands, slipping through the weakness it caused in the veil, to the land of the Living. And odds are that the Dark is going to be used to punch that weakness so hard it splits permanently. It's not just the Dead that are going to flood through, but Hell, Red. The Fallen!'

'Interesting,' said Red, apparently unmoved by Lazarus's speech.

'Not exactly how I'd describe it,' said Lazarus, wary of Red. 'All I know is that as the Keeper I have to stop this.

So, if it's all the same with you, I've a fallen angel to find and get the Black Shard from. Don't suppose you've seen him, have you? Wings? Naked? Looks pretty much the same as you?'

It was then Lazarus noticed Red's hands were dripping in blood.

27
RANK PLAGUE OF RATS

Lazarus raised his spike.

'Red . . .'

'You do not need to worry about the Black Shard,' replied Red, and stepped out of the shadows. Both his hands were slathered in dark blood, the thick stuff slipping from him like black ink from a snapped pen. In one hand was clasped the rock Lazarus had come all this way to retrieve. How was this possible? How could the one who had started him on this blood-spattered road be here at the end of it?

Lazarus raised his spike. Everything about this felt bad.

'You have it. How? Why?'

He had no idea just how powerful the Black Shard was, or what Red intended to do with it. One thing was for sure though – he didn't care how powerful Red now was; if he attacked, he'd ram the spike into him without a second thought and worry about the consequences afterwards.

'Your arrival changes things,' said Red, looking at his bloodied hand and the stone it held, like he was about to lick it clean. Taste it.

'What about the fallen angel? The one who had the Black Shard?'

Red nodded back into the shadows from where he'd walked. Lazarus looked and spotted, broken in that gloom, a smashed body.

Even in the shadows, he could see the damage that had been inflicted on it. Considering how spotless and unharmed Red looked himself, it was clear to Lazarus that the other angel hadn't stood a chance. And that Red had been more than thorough in his attack. One wing was completely severed from its body, lying away from the rest of the corpse, like the remains of a pigeon killed by a fox. Feathers everywhere. The other was bent and broken, and was still twitching a little, which unnerved Lazarus even more. This had only just happened. It was a fresh killing. The rest of the body was a masterpiece in pain. The angel's back had been ripped away, its limbs broken like a smashed doll, and its head twisted round so that its dead eyes now gazed backwards. That Red had done this, Lazarus had no doubt. But it was the ferociousness of the kill that hit him the hardest; Red had clearly shown no mercy. But why?

'If it is any consolation,' said Red, 'I warned him first. He resisted. I had no choice.'

'You tore him apart!'

Red nodded. 'He would have done the same to me. With an angel it is always best to be – well, thorough, Lazarus. I'm sure you understand.'

Looking at the evidence, Lazarus wasn't exactly convinced that the dead angel would've stood a chance anyway. But why had Red attacked with such ferocity? What the hell were his intentions?

'So now what? What are you planning to do with the Black Shard?' he asked.

The sound of Craig climbing out of the Defender echoed around them. Lazarus whipped round. 'Stay back!'

Craig wasn't given a chance to reply as Red slipped lightning quick through the air and grabbed them both.

'Shush!' he said, and placed a single finger against Lazarus's lips.

The touch of Red's finger scorched his skin and Lazarus yelled out. But before he could react and slap Red's hand away, Red spun them round and pulled him and Craig tight against his body.

'First things first, Lazarus!'

Red snapped his wings out and shot them up into the air, up through the tower. The force of it pulled Lazarus's breath from him and he gasped. Craig had already closed his eyes.

The ground dropped away. Wind stung Lazarus's eyes, first making them weep then drying the tears so his vision cleared. And at last he could see where he was, what the inside of this vast and terrible tower was actually like.

From the outside, Lazarus had been given no clue as to what the tower contained within its black stone walls. Now he knew. It was a hollow structure, miles wide, miles high. He tried to stare upwards and he caught a glimpse of a bright light far off. It was growing larger as they approached it. The surface of the walls was carved with strange symbols and writing, like that on the Black Shard. Attached to the inside of the tower were huge stone steps, each one jutting out into the centre of the tower at least a mile in length. The sheer size of everything was impossible to comprehend. It was a structure that could not exist, a thing that, under its own weight, should collapse to rubble. And yet it stood, warping and twisting reality. But that was not all, for as the three of them rose through the seemingly endless central chamber of the tower, Lazarus noticed movement on the steps. At first he thought it was just the smearing of the tears in his eyes as they sped and spun up towards wherever Red was taking him. But soon the smeared images took form as a throbbing mass of the Dead, slipping slowly up the massive steps like a thick, rank plague of rats.

'Is that what I think it is?' said Craig, at last opening his eyes to what was happening.

'You see them then,' came Red's voice, not just from behind Lazarus and Craig, but from all around them, his voice swirling in the darkness to mingle with the sound of his vast wings in flight. 'The Dead have massed not just at Simmerdale, but here also. A terrible and awesome sight, is it not?'

'What are they doing? Where are they going?'

'I am sure, Lazarus, that I do not really need to answer that.'

Red was right; he didn't. Lazarus knew exactly where they were heading and the thought twisted his gut like rope. At the top of this tower was how the Dead and the Fallen were going to smash through the veil permanently, and with cataclysmic end-of-the-world results. And every atom in his body screamed with the obvious truth, that within moments he would, once again, face the Dark . . . his *father*!

The horror of the Dark filled his mind once more, that awful weapon, created by his own mother! The thought of it brought a terrible taste to his mouth of blood and rot and fear. That his own father had been turned into this weapon was an added agony; a walking hell-storm filled with the distilled wickedness and evil of humanity, and capable of not just punching through the veil but destroying the world.

Lazarus shuddered at the thought, his brain racing for a way to escape and coming up with nothing. He knew that, like a spear thrust through someone's gut, the Dark would pierce the land of the Living at Lake Semmerwater. This would then bring about the same sequence of events as at Lake Nyos, only in this case the victims would be the tens of thousands at the festival. But before death took them all, the Dark would be upon them and the Dead themselves would slip into the still-warm bodies. And this would be the beginning of the end of all things, as the Dead swept through humanity, an unstoppable virus of decay. And over this broken world would rule the gloating Fallen!

Inexplicably, a brief candle of hope lit itself inside him. If he could get to his father, rescue him somehow, perhaps he could still put an end to all this. There was still a chance! Perhaps Arielle had been right; perhaps now it was time to truly become the Keeper.

'I still don't understand why you're here,' Lazarus said. 'Aren't you supposed to stop all this happening? You're meant to be Hell's gatekeeper! And just why is the Black Shard so important?'

Red squeezed him a little tighter and he heard Craig cough as those hugely strong arms clamped round them both. Any more so, and he'd crush them, snap them into a thousand broken bones, like that angel now far, far below.

'I was close to becoming nothing, Lazarus,' said Red. 'After sending you and Craig through the veil, I sealed it shut the only way I could; with my body.'

Lazarus noticed that the further up the tower they flew, the narrower the thing seemed, as if it was tapering to a point high above them.

'It drained me of everything,' continued Red. 'I could hear oblivion calling me; a total extinguishing of all that I had been, all that I was, all that I would ever be.'

'So what happened?'

'They came for me, Lazarus! My pets, remember?'

How could Lazarus forget; the creatures of oblivion were seared into his mind. Horrific, tumbling, twisting things of tentacles and teeth with but one purpose and one purpose only: to obey Red's every command. He'd seen what they could do, watched them rip the Dead apart like a wolf in a hen house. He didn't want to see it again. Ever.

'They rescued you?'

'Some even sacrificed themselves for me,' said Red. 'It was a beautiful thing to behold. As I am now!'

Lazarus was liking this less and less. Red was indeed beautiful, but it was an awful thing to witness, like that of Hell; a beauty he wanted to hide from for fear that staring at it too long would send him blind and crazy. And the speed they were flying at was making him dizzy.

'So what about the Black Shard?'

'It was taken a long time ago,' said Red. 'It is little more than a splinter of this tower. Yet, despite its size, it contains within it the power of this place.'

'And?'

'It is a direct link through the veil to Hell, Lazarus. I thought it had disappeared for good, but then I heard rumours, and when I met Abaddon, I knew I had to get it back. And he was my chance to do so.'

'He told me,' said Lazarus. 'You helped him . . . return.'

'And he did his job so well! Not only did he find it, he used the thing to send the Dead back!'

'Straight to Hell.'

Red shrugged. 'As good a place as any.'

Lazarus still didn't know where Red was going with this. 'But why do the Dead and the Fallen want it so badly? Why have they gone to so much trouble to find it and bring it back?'

'Because,' said Red, 'they did not want it to fall into the wrong hands.'

'Whose?'

Red's eyes burned. 'Mine!'

They burst from the top of the tower. Where Lazarus had seen walls and the Dead climbing that stair, he now saw the sky, only it was empty, void of star and moon. A black endlessness that when you stared into it for too long would make you feel like you were about to topple forwards into it and fall for an eternity choking on the sound of your own lonely, endless screams.

Silent and gentle as falling snow, Red brought them down to land on a vast granite platform. It stretched out at all angles, covering the entire circumference of the tower like the scattered remains of a shattered star. It was huge, but nothing like the size of the tower's base, confirming what Lazarus had noticed as they had flown upwards, that the structure did indeed taper inwards, like a spike.

Lazarus could see at its centre the dark hole they had flown out from, leading back down the spiral staircase filled with the Dead into the terrifying heights of the tower, at the bottom of which was Arielle's Defender. He briefly wondered just what Arielle would say when – *if* – they got back and told her that her faithful truck was still in Hell.

The platform was crowded. But not with the Dead. They were standing waiting at the top of the spiral staircase; Lazarus could see through the hole in the centre of the platform. The figures on the platform were something entirely different. And he knew immediately what they were.

'Beautiful, are they not?' said Red, releasing his grip on Lazarus and Craig, letting them slip to the cold, smooth stone floor. 'My brothers and sisters – the Fallen!'

Lazarus couldn't tell how many there were, and he didn't want to know. That they were there in front of him was enough, with more and more coming into land, some with burns and singed wings, and Lazarus remembered how Craig had spotted the Fallen circling the tower like vultures. Lusting after the stink of death.

But that wasn't the worst of it. Because dragging itself towards the hole in the centre of the platform, towards the thick queue of expectant Dead, was the Dark. Lazarus knew it was the reason why none of the Fallen had noticed them; they were all staring at it, their wings beating a slow breeze to skip across the platform and tumble off its edge.

The Dark was vast, and pulsed with an almost electrical buzz that crackled its shimmering surface with white lines of lightning. It was all colours and none, a featureless thing that stretched out thick tentacles of itself around the hole in the platform and up into the sky, as if it was blindly searching for something that only it knew lay out there. And Lazarus knew that somewhere at its centre was his dad; the sole reason for him being here, the one thing he'd held on to through all the horrors, that at the end of it they'd be able to start anew, get to know each other as a father and son, *live* . . .

Ruining that hopeful image with all the keenness of a surgeon's blade, a terrible thought sliced through Lazarus and he snatched himself away from Red, dragging Craig with him, and raised his spike. Not that he stood a chance here if a fight kicked off, surrounded, as he was, by creatures who could snap him in half just by looking at him.

'You've switched sides, haven't you!' he yelled, pointing at Red with his spike. 'You've ditched everything you stood for and betrayed us!'

Red moved forward, his wings folded against his back, his hands palms down as though trying to keep Lazarus calm. Some of the Fallen had noticed them and they didn't look happy about their arrival.

'Lazarus, you must listen to me—'

'Back off!' Lazarus shouted, and jabbed at Red with the spike to make him stop. 'I don't know what that Black Shard does, and I don't really care. All I do know is that I have to stop this!'

He pointed at the Dark. Below it, the Dead were screaming and howling. It reminded Lazarus of what they'd witnessed in Simmerdale. 'I have to get my father back! And if that means killing you right here, right now, I will, you hear me?'

Lazarus was going to say something else, but a shock wave blasted out from the centre of the platform and sent him and Craig tumbling.

28

HELL ON EARTH

Lazarus tried to keep on his feet, but it was no good. He fell forwards into Red, stumbling at first, the edge of the platform so close he thought they were going to crash over it at any second. But just steps away from it, they both fell to the floor with a heavy thud and Lazarus heard Red groan with it. Then a warmth spread down his arm.

'Lazarus . . .'

The spike was embedded in Red up to its handle, right through his stomach and out the other side. Blood gushed out of the wound and as Lazarus pulled himself away and tried to stand up, he slipped in the pool spreading out from Red and fell to his knees again.

'Red? I didn't mean to—'

A gurgling laugh dribbled from Red. Craig was at

Lazarus's side and helped him to his feet, the blood passing between them like a rash.

'What happened?'

Lazarus didn't know what he was feeling now. He was angry, but he was also upset. He hadn't meant to stab Red! And he could see more of the Fallen turning now. Some were howling, others were pointing. They all looked pissed as hell.

'It was an accident!' he yelled. 'I fell! We all did!'

Red managed to struggle into a sitting position. Then he reached down for the spike and yanked it from his body, tossing it back to Lazarus. A fresh spew of blood gurgled out of the hole left behind. Red tried to stand but fell to his knees.

'The Dark, Lazarus – look!'

Lazarus whipped round from Red and saw the Dark poised directly above the swollen mass of the Dead, its thick tentacles attaching it around the circumference of the hole in the centre of the platform. For a moment, the Fallen and the Dead were still, watching, waiting. Then, silently and slowly, the Dark started to twist and turn, like melted candy. As it stretched up into the featureless sky its insides began to spin and whirl and soon it was a ferocious and violent vortex. With screams of delight, the Dead began to be sucked up into it, their bodies knocking against each other, sending splashes of blood down on to the platform and up into the Dark itself, streaking it red. As more and more were sucked up, it became impossible to see individual figures; the Dead had become a stream, flushing out of the hole from the spiral staircase and up into the Dark, which was growing, stretching higher, like it was feeding on them and getting fat on their rotten flesh.

Lazarus snapped back to Red as the tower shuddered and he felt it start to push upwards. 'What's it doing? How do we stop it?'

'The Black Shard, Lazarus,' Red coughed, leaning on his hands and nodding to the splinter of rock lying in his own blood. 'Give it to me!'

'The Dark, Red! Tell me what to do!'

Some of the Fallen were approaching now. They were all carrying spikes like the one Lazarus had in his hand. He was reminded then of its origins, that it had been forged to be wielded by an angel. It was a terrible weapon.

He didn't want to imagine just how terrible in the hands of those now approaching.

Another blood-spattered cough.

'You are the Keeper, Lazarus! Your job is to stop the Dark! My job is to rule Hell! Now, the Black Shard! Please!'

Lazarus didn't move. And still the tower rose upwards. Around it the sky was splitting open, ripping apart, like the tower was smashing its way through sheets of glass. Lightning streaked the darkness and the tower shook as it rose, almost like it would soon crumble and fall. A great hole was opening up around it as it pushed on and Lazarus could see water on all sides falling away from them, like he was now inside a waterfall. A dark sky of stars lay far above. The tower was breaking its way through Lake Semmerwater!

Red used his wings to help him balance as he pulled himself up to stand. The feathers were stained and dripping with his own dark blood. Beyond the platform Lazarus could now see the lake and the valley spreading out below them, and the festival. Or what was left of it. The thousands who had turned up to party for the weekend were lying on the ground, unconscious. The gas from the lake, he realised! Everything Matthew had said was true! The force of the tower pushing through must have caused the lake to explode and gas to swamp the valley. Now, with all those fresh warm bodies lying waiting, all the Dead had to do was slip into them unhindered.

'The Fallen have been behind this all along!' Red called to Lazarus, his voice catching breathless in his throat. 'They used the Dead to their own ends; to create the Dark to do what you are now seeing and break Hell through the veil! I was blind to it. They wanted me out of the picture; the fact I managed to almost do that myself when I rescued you and Craig was, to them, a bonus!'

Lazarus was too busy staring at what was happening beyond the tower. The Dark, its job now done in pulling the tower through, was forming a great oily cloud in the sky, and from it rained the Dead. And when they landed on the festival site, they crawled into the nearest body they could find with howls of delight. But where were Abaddon and Arielle, thought Lazarus? What had happened to them?

Red spoke again.

'The Fallen sent the Black Shard through the veil long ago. They used it to slip the Dead through, to prepare the way, unseen by me. I retrieved it and with Abaddon's help used it to try and undo what they had done. But not enough it seems.'

'But why do they need it now?' asked Lazarus, turning from the awful site outside the tower. The approaching Fallen were closer still, their wings outstretched now, and they looked ready to tear them all apart. 'Isn't the Dark enough with the veil weakened by what Abaddon did to Simmerdale?'

Red sighed and for a split second Lazarus thought he was about to pitch forward, dead.

'Yes. And no. Think, Lazarus, what would happen if that Black Shard was to become a part of the Dark?'

Lazarus hadn't a clue.

'It would not only open the veil and allow Hell through, but build a permanent bridge! This would not simply be about the Dead and the Fallen raining death and destruction down on humanity; this would be Hell on Earth! In the literal sense! It would be fixed there, permanently nailed to it. And there would be no hope after. No hope at all!'

The enormity of Red's words threatened to crush Lazarus on the spot. His voice snared in his throat. 'But after all that's happened, and when I saw you with it, I assumed you'd switched sides! I thought that was why you had brought us up here – to hand it over! And us!'

'No,' said Red. 'I brought you up here because I had no choice. I did not expect you. I was going to destroy the Black Shard and throw myself into the Dark. I would not be able to stop it, but perhaps I could slow it down a little, buy you some time.'

Lazarus paused as he tried to take in Red's admission of self-sacrifice. 'So now what?'

A roar from the approaching Fallen caught all of their attention. Lazarus turned from Red to see them lift from the platform, their wings beating slow and hard. They were no longer so beautiful, their feathers shimmering like black metal, their faces pulled into nightmare visions of hate and loathing.

'We have but one option,' said Red.

Lazarus was given no time to react as Red pulled

enough strength into his weakened body to grab him and Craig, snatch the Black Shard from the pool of his own blood, then slip backwards off the platform into the air.

Lazarus's scream was lost to the wind as they fell. Red's arms gripped him, but their strength was fading. It wouldn't be long before he'd slip free. Not that it would matter; in a few moments they'd hit the lake and then he'd drown.

Red was wriggling around, Lazarus assumed to try and make some use of his wings to stay their fall. He had no idea if it was doing any good; all he could hear was the rushing of the wind and the fluttering of those feathers. And they were spinning too, like a plane out of control heading for a collision with the ground. Lazarus knew he should've been more scared of the death that was only seconds away, but he'd become so accustomed to it that all he felt was disappointment. Everything he'd done had been a waste of time.

The spinning ended with a thunderous crash and Lazarus's world filled with icy water. They were in the lake. This was it: the end!

Lazarus couldn't breathe, couldn't swim. He caught a

brief glimpse of Red, of Craig. His legs and arms fought uselessly against the water and he sunk even further. The cold stabbed at him like a million pins and his whole body started to go numb. Any moment now he'd pass out and never wake up.

Something clawed at his neck and Lazarus tried to knock it away. It came again, like it was trying to bite into him, and no amount of spinning and twisting did any good to get rid of it. Whatever it was, it yanked hard and Lazarus shot up through the water. He tasted air, breathed hard and came down with a thump on sodden wood. When he opened his eyes, Lazarus saw his rescuer: Abaddon! His hand was in the water and with another yank he pulled Craig from the lake and dropped him in the rowboat next to Lazarus.

'Red . . .' spluttered Lazarus, managing just one word as he coughed up a gurgle of lake water.

In reply, Abaddon looked up to the sky. Lazarus followed his line of sight to see something drop out of nowhere and into the lake like a missile. Water exploded upwards and fell down on them like a crashing wave as Abaddon began to row them back to shore. The water exploded again, and this time Lazarus saw what was the cause: it was Arielle, and in her arms was Red.

Arielle flew overhead and to the shore, resting Red down gently. Abaddon was as silent as ever. Craig was coughing and shivering badly. And the world around them was total chaos.

The foul and terrifying tower was still rising out of the water behind them, its edges now brushing up against the lake's shore, dragging great furrows of earth and stone up into the air, the water steaming into vast plumes of mist, or falling like rain. The dark was flowing out from the platform at the top, risen so high now that Lazarus could hardly see it, but not just as a cloud above it, but as a thick tar running down its walls. And in it he could see the Dead, twisting and turning and bubbling, lusting after the promise of a body to occupy!

'You look better than I expected,' said Lazarus, looking at Abaddon though it was more than a little like sitting in a boat with the ferryman on the river Styx.

'That is Arielle's doing,' Abaddon replied. 'Without the Black Shard I am still more fragile than before, but it's power remains in me, knitted into the preserved flesh of my corpse.'

Lazarus looked over to where the festival was now nothing more than a mass of the Dead going crazy for the bodies lying on the floor.

'What happened?'

'It was as you said: the gas from the lake burst out. Arielle only just managed to fly out of range in time. I was not affected. We were at the commune when it happened.'

'A limnic explosion,' stuttered Craig, his mouth shivering like mad. 'Unbelievable!'

Lazarus rested a hand on his friend then stared over Abaddon's shoulder to the shore. Red was lying on the ground, unconscious, maybe even dead, Arielle kneeling with his head in her lap. And from behind him, the horrifying shadow of the tower stretched outwards, blanketing the world in a black chill. But then something caught his eye; a movement behind Arielle and Red as two shadows silently approached.

With a shiver, he looked back to Abaddon, a quivering finger raised. 'So you didn't find Mary then?'

Abaddon shook his head. 'No. She was not there. We searched everywhere, but nothing. Not a trace! But I will not give up, Keeper, of that you can be sure.'

'Well, I've got news for you,' said Lazarus, unable to hide the desperate fear in his voice.

By now the shadows had taken form and he could see them clearly. And still Arielle and Red had noticed nothing.

Abaddon's eyeless face twisted in confusion. 'You found her? Where, boy? In Hell?'

Lazarus shook his head. 'No, Abaddon, not in Hell. Mary's here; she's found you instead!'

29

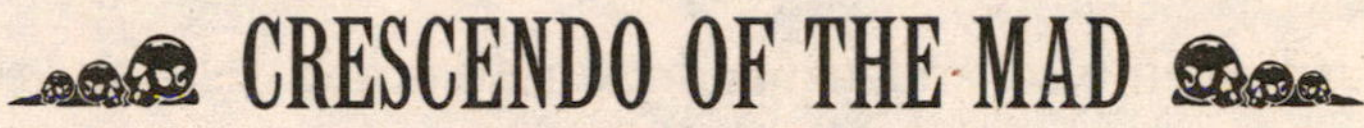

CRESCENDO OF THE MAD

Abaddon snatched his head round to the shore, caught sight of the man and young girl Lazarus was pointing at, and roared like a man witnessing his world fall to pieces despite his best efforts to prevent it.

Abaddon's war cry swept across the water, made Arielle pull away from patching up Red to stare at them across the water.

'Behind you!' Lazarus screamed, jumping to his feet, but too late Arielle responded as the man attacked.

'Move it!' yelled Lazarus, as the boat swayed and nearly sent him back into the water and caused Craig to slip from the bench seat into the water swilling around in the bottom of the boat.

From deep within the loss and pain he'd endured for centuries, the dead priest dragged such a burst of energy that his sculling almost kicked the boat out of the water as he raced them back to the shore.

All Lazarus could do was watch as Arielle, caught off guard, stumbled and tripped over Red and fell into the lake, her hands desperately searching for the hilt of her sword and her pistol.

'What's wrong with you? Can't you go any faster?' Lazarus shouted again at Abaddon.

'I am trying to!' answered Abaddon, a reek of death on his breath. 'Do not distract me!'

Arielle was now on her feet, leaning on her sword. With her other hand, she raised the pistol, but the man with Mary stepped over the unconscious Red and slapped it away into the shallows. Mary, though, was just standing, as if she was observing a fight in a school playground and wondering whether or not to go and tell the teacher.

Nearer now, Lazarus recognised the man as the one he and Arielle had seen drop off Mary and the fallen angel at Matthew's camper van. But who was he? And why was he with Mary?

Arielle struggled to stay on her feet as she retreated from the man, her sword up now and ready. Then her feet caught on something and she fell backwards, landing awkwardly with a yell. But the yell was soon replaced by a squeal as the man launched into her with a kick so powerful it lifted her off the ground to land hard in the water. He came at her again. She raised a hand to stop him, but the kick came anyway, and once more she was airborne, this time landing like her pistol in the lake.

Lazarus was about to yell at Abaddon again when the bottom of the boat grated against the lake bed. He didn't wait for an invitation and leapt out of the boat like a gazelle, the spike in his hand.

The man barely had time to register that Lazarus was approaching before the spike sliced across his stomach and, in the same movement, he found himself being thrown to the ground with such force that his face smashed into the pebbled beach and ruined his teeth.

Lazarus brought himself to a halt, breathing deep, a wildness flowing through him from the drawing of blood. As he dragged himself to his feet and turned to face the man he could now see the awful splendour of the tower as it ruptured the world. It seemed even more awful here than it had in Hell, like a great burned tree scorched with a heat that would soon spread outwards and consume everything that lay beyond it. Just off to his right, Red was still on the floor, his chest heaving as he pulled in hacked, pained breaths. To his left, Arielle was back on her feet again, her lips flecked with her own blood as she coughed like a dying smoker. She raised her sword, then having spotted something in the water, dropped down to retrieve her pistol and took aim.

'Do it!' said Lazarus. 'Drop him so we can get on with finishing this!'

'He's human,' said Arielle. 'Not dead. Not yet anyway. Your call, Keeper!'

The news struck Lazarus like a football to the face. Slicing the Dead to pieces he hadn't a problem with, but using his spike against someone occupied by the Dead appalled him.

The man stood up and spat teeth and blood into the air.

'We've been waiting for this moment,' he said. 'You cannot stop us!'

'I wouldn't be so sure of that,' answered Lazarus,

now trying to get close enough to the man to evict the Dead inside him.

The man laughed, but it sounded like opening the door on a cathedral filled with the insane; a haunting, manic crescendo of the mad.

It was cut short by a clatter of thunder. Only it wasn't thunder, it was the sound of flint striking steel and the sparking of gunpowder.

Lazarus stepped back in shock as the man shuddered, surprise in his eyes, then dropped to his knees. Standing in the space he had occupied was Abaddon, a smoking flintlock pistol in each hand.

'He's human . . .' said Lazarus, staring at Abaddon, still horrified at his own act of violence, but now shocked to see the cold efficiency of the dead priest in full flow.

Abaddon said nothing, just stepped over the man and walked towards Lazarus, throwing the pistols away and replacing them with two more from the inner folds of his jacket.

'Out of my way, Keeper.'

Lazarus stayed his ground, all too aware now that behind him was Abaddon's daughter.

'It's not her, Abaddon,' he said, trying to keep his voice calm. 'It's just a shell!'

'He's right, Abaddon,' Arielle spoke out in agreement. 'That is not your daughter, not any more! It can't be, and deep down you know it!'

But Abaddon wasn't listening and Lazarus knew there was no way any of them would get through to him now, not until this was over. He stepped aside.

Abaddon continued towards his daughter. He was almost upon her when, with almost childish glee, she turned and skipped away into the darkness. Abaddon followed.

They were one man down. Lazarus attempted to get to Craig, who was struggling to pull himself out of the boat, when the man who had attacked Arielle sat up and vomited. His head twisted round to face Lazarus.

'We are not yet gone, Keeper!' he hissed.

Lazarus gave the man no warning and closed the space between them in a single jump. He rammed the spike into the ground at his feet.

'That's because I haven't finished,' he said, and clamped his hands on either side of the man's face.

The sensation of touching an occupied body sent a shock wave through Lazarus so harsh that he arched his back and screamed. Even if he'd wanted to pull his hands away, he knew full well it would've been pointless trying; they were attached now until the Dead were evicted. Or he perished.

Lazarus forced himself back in control and looked down at the man whose whole body was shaking violently now, a bloody froth flowing from his nose, his mouth, the corners of his eyes. He tried to claw at Lazarus, but there was no strength in it and Lazarus would not be taken off task; he was the Keeper and no stinking Dead was going to get in his way. Not any more.

With a final effort, Lazarus dug deep, found the Dead hooked inside the man like giant tapeworms, and ripped them free, pulling them out of him as he wrenched himself away to land on the ground on his back.

The man let out a scream that sounded like he'd been ripped in half, but when Lazarus looked up, he was still in one piece. However, something awful was happening. At first it looked like he was just trying to stand on his feet again, but quickly Lazarus realised he wasn't trying to stand on them at all, he was being dragged; something was forcing him to his feet, pulling him up until not even his toes touched the ground.

'What's happening?' Lazarus shouted to Arielle.

Arielle had no answer, just stared.

With a final yell, the man's arms were wrenched out straight, and for a moment he just hung there on an invisible cross. Then, almost as though his body had become a part of the sun, light and heat broke from him, spraying outwards in great looping waves, and any screams he had left were lost to the roar of energy leaving his body.

The light and head stopped. The man dropped to the ground like a sack of coal.

Lazarus crawled over. Against the odds, the man was still alive, his chest slowly rising and falling, a faint breath escaping him. Not knowing quite what to do, he slipped his hand under his shoulders and lifted him into his lap. Arielle and Craig approached.

'My boys . . . where are my sons?'

'He's alive after that?' said Craig. 'He can't be!'

The wound Lazarus himself had inflicted looked rough

and deep. As for the bullet wounds from Abaddon, he could feel a trickle of blood on his legs. Yet he was alive and Lazarus was overcome with relief.

'I thought I'd killed him,' he said.

'So did Abaddon,' added Arielle. 'But the Dead look after the bodies they occupy. These are bad wounds, yes, but not life-threatening and I can heal them. Had they been, that would've been different.'

The man coughed as Arielle rested her hands on him.

'Where am I?'

'What do you remember?' asked Arielle, the wounds healing slowly.

The man shuddered and shivered.

'Do you remember your name?'

The man's brow creased and he said, 'James . . . yes, that's it. James Barton. I was on holiday. Rented a cabin by a lake.'

'That's it? Nothing else?'

'I don't understand.'

The man's words had jogged something in Lazarus's memory and he took over from Arielle. 'When were you on holiday? Do you remember the date?'

Again the man looked confused, but finally answered.

'That's five years ago,' said Lazarus glancing at Arielle. 'And remember Willie? He mentioned that city bloke who bought up the cabins, set up the commune? He said his name was James Barton.'

'There was this girl,' said James, suddenly sounding more lucid, but his eyes glazing, like he was somewhere else now, reliving a long-forgotten dream. 'I was down by the lake when I spotted her. She was just floating there in this white dress!'

'What did you do?'

'She was so cold,' said James. 'I thought she was dead, prayed she wasn't. If I hadn't been there . . .'

James went silent, but was soon talking again.

'I took the girl back to my cabin, covered her in a duvet, called an ambulance. But I couldn't work out how she'd got there! What the hell was she doing on the lake on her own? And it was early morning! It didn't make sense!'

James went quiet again, but Lazarus pressed on.

'What happened?'

'She . . . she woke up,' he whispered, like he was afraid someone would overhear. 'She seemed OK until she said something weird about the air smelling alive. I didn't think anything of it, guessed she was delirious with the cold. I asked where her parents were but she just kept saying they were coming, they were coming, they all were!'

'Who were coming?' asked Lazarus. 'Her parents?'

James screamed and pulled at his face.

'Her fingers!' he yelled out, tears streaming now. 'Oh, God, those fingers!'

Lazarus didn't want to ask, but knew he had to.

"What about them, James? What happened?'

'She . . . her hands . . . she clasped the side of my head!' James grabbed at Lazarus, desperation in his eyes. 'I couldn't move! I could smell burning! Then, when I tried to pull her off, her fingers . . . they were in my skin! Oh, God, they were actually in my skin, you hear me? Crawling down my cheeks! And something was pouring out of them into me! Awful things! Nightmares and darkness and . . .'

James broke down with a sob.

'Abaddon's daughter did this,' said Arielle. 'Whatever was done to her all those years ago was the start of everything happening now.'

'But if she was occupied by one of the Dead, what was

she doing floating on the lake?'

'The Black Shard,' said Arielle. 'She's been using it to ferry the Dead across the veil all this time back from the damned village of Simmerdale. And five years ago the Dead and the Fallen put into place the final part of their plan; to set up a permanent base here and bring Hell crashing through!'

James's sobbing quietened and Lazarus noticed that the world had taken on an eerie silence, like it was preparing itself for a killer storm. He glanced over to the festival fields.

'Why's it so quiet? What's happening?'

The light show continued crazily, but the place was silent. No music. No cheering.

'The gas,' said Arielle. 'It hit so fast no one stood a chance. The place fell silent in a moment. It was a dreadful sight, Lazarus. Then the Dark came and brought with it the Dead.'

As if in answer, a moan crawled from deep inside the silence, the sound of thousands of voices all suddenly moving with singular purpose and intent.

Craig pointed down the road that led from the lake

to the festival. 'I don't want to worry you,' he said, 'but look . . .'

Far off, a thick crowd was advancing down the road towards them. A flood of bodies now occupied by the Dead! And they were coming at such a speed, racing and stumbling and throwing themselves along, that Lazarus knew in minutes they would be swamped.

Then Craig spoke again and his words snatched Lazarus's breath away.

'It's Clair,' he said. 'And she's leading them!'

30
ALL WARS HAVE THEIR VICTIMS

The vision in front of Lazarus jarred with the memory of the person he now saw coming towards them. Clair was a nurse, a friend and someone who had only got involved in this because she knew Craig. But to see her now, twisted beyond all recognition by whatever evil occupied her body, she was almost unrecognisable.

'They'll be on us in minutes,' he said. 'Clair even sooner!'

A cough sounded from behind and as one they turned to see Red roll on to his side and vomit out a flood of blood-stained water.

'He's awake!' Arielle whispered desperately, and rushed over to him. Lazarus saw tears in her eyes.

'Arielle,' Red smiled through cracked, bleeding

lips, his voice no more than a breath. He then gently touched her cheek with a pale, shaking finger. 'It has been a long time!'

Arielle reached out and held his hand, smiled a little. 'I thought you were gone,' she said. 'I pulled you from the lake, but you didn't stir, wouldn't wake!'

Lazarus coughed to get some attention and nodded back to Clair and the zombie horde approaching. Except these weren't zombies, they were worse; the Living filled with the Dead.

'I think we need to save the big reunion till later.'

James Barton had stopped sobbing now and was just sitting quietly, rocking back and forth.

Red sat up and sucked in a pained breath, holding his stomach like he was trying to stop his guts from spilling out. Arielle helped him steady himself. Something fell from the folds of his tattered, bloody wings. It was the Black Shard.

'You brought it back?' said Lazarus, his voice shaking.

'Where is Abaddon?' asked Red, ignoring Lazarus. 'He will have need of it now.'

'But it has to be destroyed!' said Lazarus. 'You told

me – that's what you said, Arielle, right?'

'That was then,' the angel replied. 'This is now. But Abaddon is not here, Red. He is on the hunt again.'

A howl screeched out and Lazarus saw Clair break away from the swarming crowd and start running. Would he have to fight a friend once more? First Craig and now Clair? He walked over to retrieve his spike from where he'd rammed it in the ground before evicting the Dead from James.

The thorns in the handle of the spike slipped through his hand and out the other side. A cry, like a pack of wolves being run over by a truck, hurled itself at Lazarus. He looked up to see Mary come flying backwards out of the darkness to tumble into Clair and send them both sprawling. The crowd stopped dead and stared as though without Clair in front they weren't quite sure what to do next.

Abaddon emerged from the darkness a moment later.

Lazarus reacted, charging over to Clair before Abaddon had a chance to go after her too. But he was more concerned with Mary, who was already on her feet and racing back to join the throng from the festival. Abaddon made chase but a wall of flesh closed up behind her. His fury tore from him with a roar like an earthquake.

Lazarus ignored Abaddon and approached Clair. She was on her knees, cut and bleeding from the fall. He wanted to say something, warn her about what he was about to do, but there was no time. He reached out to clasp her head with his hands and evict the Dead inside her. But Clair responded first, sweeping round at him in the same movement that brought her to her feet, caught him hard in the face, and knocked him to the ground. Lazarus was up as quick as he'd been felled.

'It's me, Clair!' he shouted, holding a hand up to keep her back. 'Lazarus, remember? Don't listen to the things inside you! Ignore them! Fight them!'

Clair did nothing of the sort. She launched herself at Lazarus, driving her head into his stomach, knocking the wind from him completely. Coughing, he stood up, but she did the same again. Lazarus knew his only chance was to use the spike, but he risked killing her if he did. He climbed to his feet, Clair came for him, he stepped to one side to dodge her, but she was too quick and again he was on the ground. Then, as he rolled over on to his back, she leapt at him. Lazarus raised his hands to protect himself and to try and catch Clair and throw her off.

Too late he realised he was still holding the spike.

Clair's body came to a shocking stop as the spike sunk into her chest and burst out of her back. She didn't even scream.

For a moment, Lazarus was too shocked to react. Clair clawed at him, caught his cheek and drew blood. Then he leaned to one side and gave the spike a pull, releasing Clair from the blade. She dropped to the ground next to him and Lazarus backed off, afraid she would attack again, horrified by the wound he had just inflicted. Clair sat up, looked like she was going to come for him once more, then just as quickly, dropped back to the ground as something awful started to push out of the wound.

First came the hands, dozens of them reaching out, gripping Clair's flesh and pulling. Then came the heads, all squashed together like the seeds of a pomegranate, quickly followed by torsos twisted together like tangled sausages. Then at last it was free. It looked over to Lazarus, the heads staring at him, straining to get a look.

'You broke her,' the thing said. 'So I will

have you now instead.'

'I doubt that,' came a voice from behind Lazarus. Abaddon stepped forward, crushed the creature into the ground with a boot, then raised a blunderbuss and fired.

Lazarus wiped gore from his face as the creature slumped at his feet and started to dissolve. Abaddon said nothing more and walked over to Red, Craig and Arielle. Lazarus though was staring at Clair. Amazingly, she was still breathing.

Lazarus scrambled across to her and shouted for Arielle. He took Clair's head in his hands, desperate to know what to do, but feeling utterly helpless. The angel bounded over, but when she arrived, the look in her eyes said more than enough.

'I don't believe you!' Lazarus screamed. 'You have to be able to heal her, like you healed me, remember? You can do this! I know it!'

Arielle shook her head. 'It's not just her body that's damaged,' she said, 'but her soul. And I can't do anything about that. We have to let her go.'

'No!' shouted Lazarus. 'Heal her! Do it! I'm ordering you to!'

Arielle reached out to him, but he pulled away.

'The eviction was too violent,' explained Arielle, her voice soft and calm. 'The Dead had to leave because her body was dying from the wound inflicted by the spike. They evicted themselves, Lazarus. And when they do that, they don't leave clean; they make sure everything's a mess, unsurvivable.'

Clair's body shuddered. Her breaths grew short.

'But you're an angel! And I'm the Keeper, for God's sake! What's the point in any of this if we can't even save someone who shouldn't have been here in the first place?'

'All wars have their victims, Lazarus.'

'That's total crap and you know it!'

Lazarus had more to say but a shudder from Clair caught his attention. When he looked down, her eyes were open. 'I'm sorry,' he whispered.

Clair's eyes slipped shut and her body fell still.

'She's gone, Lazarus,' said Arielle. 'We will mourn her later, if we survive.'

Lazarus rested Clair's head on the ground and stood up. Behind him was the Tower of Hell and above it the swirling mass of the Dark, spilling down its sides to infect the Earth. In front of him were the Dead themselves, desperate to run riot in their new bodies, spread their cancer through humanity. And swarming in the air like wasps, were the Fallen. Hell was no longer coming, it was already here.

'The Dark,' Lazarus said, wiping tears from his eyes. 'We destroy that, we kill the hold that the tower has on this place. And there's still a chance I can save my dad.'

'I don't know, Lazarus,' Arielle replied. 'I'm not sure I know anything any more.'

James, his wounds all but gone thanks to Arielle, was now with Red and the others, and despite the tiredness and confusion on his face, was clasping a spiked club, no doubt something Abaddon had given him for protection. Craig tried to mutter something about Clair, but choked. Abaddon seemed different. His strength had clearly returned. Lazarus knew then it was a result of the Black Shard back inside him. Red had returned it whole to the undeed priest, for good or ill.

Lazarus ignored Arielle's doubt. He'd nearly lost Craig and had just watched Clair die. He wasn't about to lose his dad as well, even if that meant going back to the tower.

Red said, 'We must take Hell back to where it belongs.'

Lazarus nodded grimly, teeth clenched shut, his mind playing over and over Clair's last breath. It was all he could do to hold it together.

'And I must go back with it.'

'No!' gasped Arielle. 'You can't go back!'

There was more emotion in Arielle's voice than Lazarus had expected.

'It was you, wasn't it?' he said, now looking to Red. 'During the war, it was you who Arielle was sent behind the lines to befriend!'

'You have a keen eye, Lazarus,' smiled Red. 'But watch or you'll cut yourself on what you find.'

Lazarus was unmoved by Red's thinly disguised threat. He half wondered if anything would ever truly move him again.

'I am Hell's gatekeeper,' said Red. 'It needs me.'

Arielle went to say something but a look from Red sent her quiet. He then stood up and reached a hand out to Lazarus. 'We must do this together, Keeper. You must stop the Dark, halt the Dead for good, and I must take Hell back to where it belongs! It is the only way. Agreed?'

Lazarus shook Red's hand.

'And the veil? I thought only death could seal it?'

Red pointed towards the tower. 'That thing,' he said, 'is the very essence of death, and on death it is built!'

'You're speaking in riddles again,' said Lazarus. 'We don't have time.'

Red stepped even closer. 'Each and every brick is inscribed with the name of someone who has passed over. Some to a better place, some to— well, you know of where I speak, Lazarus! And so the tower grows, and so it ever shall, until all things are ended.'

A howl rose like that of wind riding a storm to rip trees from their roots. The Dead were on the march.

Lazarus looked at the rest of the group. 'We're going to need a diversion.'

'You sure this will work?'

Lazarus was standing with Arielle, the spike clasped tight in his left hand. Abaddon and Craig were between them and the Dead, who were growing restless. But something was stopping them attacking.

Lazarus stared at the priest as he faced off the Dead. 'Why haven't they come for us? What are they waiting for?'

'Abaddon's reputation goes before him,' said Arielle. 'Remember that he now has all of the Black Shard, not just a part of it. The Dead fear him.'

Red said, 'Are you ready?'

'In every way no,' replied Lazarus, 'but the Dark is the one thing that's keeping that tower, the Damned and the Dead here in the land of the Living, isn't it? If I can slash my way through the Dark to Dad and free him, then it should fail.'

'You sound confident.'

'If you've a better plan, let me know.'

'I'm not really sure you can call this a plan,' Arielle replied. 'Suicidal, insane, last chance . . . but plan?' She shook her head and said no more.

Lazarus was pleased. He was the Keeper. He was the only one with the power to bring the Dark down. He hadn't been able to save Clair, but he still had that slim chance of rescuing his father. And it all hinged on the diversion. He looked to Red.

'You understand what we're going to do?'

Red nodded and as he did so both his own and Arielle's wings cracked the air like whips. 'I will go in first,' he said. 'I am hoping that the Fallen hate their jailer more than they want to kill you.'

'Me too,' said Lazarus. 'If you can't draw them off, then this plan's dead already.'

'Oh, they will follow me,' said Red, a sneering grin cutting sharp and deadly across his face like the glimmer of broken glass. 'And I will lead them back into the tower if I can. That way, I will at least have a chance to call for some help.'

That was the one part of the plan Lazarus really didn't like. Red had jumped at the chance to cause the diversion. His enthusiasm for it had been matched only by the fire in his eyes when he'd said that, if he could, he would call for his 'pets'. Not only was such a term utterly inappropriate for something so terrifyingly efficient in dealing out relentless violence, but more than that, Lazarus had experienced first hand what Red and those creatures could do. He had a sense that it could very easily get out of control.

Arielle said, 'I will drop you on the platform and protect you as best I can, but then it is down to you. If you are unable to rescue your father . . .'

'I know,' said Lazarus, knowing Arielle's unspoken words were his worst fear, that if rescuing his dad was impossible, he would have to destroy the Dark with him still inside it.

But destroy it how?

He looked down at his hands, the hands of a Keeper. Like his father before him, they had the power in them to rip the Dead from the living. But would they be enough to blast the Dark from existence? He'd soon find out.

With a breath deep enough to burst his lungs, Lazarus nodded to Arielle and Red. The next thing he knew, he was airborne, Arielle holding him tight, and Red flying ahead directly into a gathering horde of fallen angels as thick and black as a swarm of locusts set against a black sky burning.

31

HIDEOUS SPINNING VORTEX

Arielle's grip on him was so tight, and their speed so ferocious, Lazarus could hardly breathe. The lake was far below them, but he could still make out the crowd of thousands from the festival standing like an army awaiting its final orders. And standing waiting for them were three figures; Abaddon, Craig and James. What hope they stood when the Dead attacked he did not know. It would do him no good to dwell on it either. So he turned away and looked ahead and into the very jaws of Hell.

'Lazarus,' said Arielle, bringing him out of his thoughts, 'if ever there was a good time to start praying, now would be it.'

Lazarus saw Red hovering, his great black wings sweeping slowly back and forth in the air to keep him aloft. Coming at him from high above, like a great flock of eagles, their wings swept back, were the Fallen. How many he didn't know, couldn't even guess at, but it was more than enough to make him think this whole plan was about to die in front of his eyes. Because against that many, he couldn't see how Red would have a chance, even in Hell.

With the crashing, crunching sound of a motorway pile-up, the Fallen smashed into Red, their great black shadow smudging him from the sky in a second. Then from inside that shadow, Red exploded, and the Fallen followed him, first high up above the tower, and then crashing down into it. At the same time, a roar from the ground shot upwards and Lazarus gazed down just in time to see the three on the ground disappear from sight in a flood of the Dead. They were on their own now, he thought, and there was nothing he could do about it except get his part of the job done. And at least the first part of the plan had worked; Red had managed to be sufficient bait to drag the Fallen away and back down through the tower. And if he returned, Lazarus knew it would be with his pets at his side, the creatures of oblivion.

Lazarus wasn't given a chance to think about it any

more, as Arielle suddenly accelerated at such a rate his head was pushed down into his shoulders. All he could do was trust Arielle and hope that she didn't drop him. It was a long way down, and in a sky filled with the Fallen, he didn't really think his chances of being rescued were that high.

The platform at the top of the tower came into view. Arielle shot over it, checking for a place to land, then, with a hard bank round to the left, swept her wings back and dropped them out of the sky and down on to the platform. They landed with an extraordinary gentleness that was hard to believe after the speeds they had just been doing.

'You look exhausted,' said Lazarus.

'Flying is all very well,' said Arielle, 'but it drains me more than it should. I have been on Earth so long now that my wings have forgotten how to do what they're designed for. There is not much call for it. I do it only when all other options have been extinguished.'

He was about to check if she was going to be all right, when out of nowhere something knocked them both off their feet. Arielle was back up in the blink of an eye, her wings extended like a protective shield in front of Lazarus.

'Move it, Laz!'

Lazarus scrambled to his feet, his spike cleaving a gouge in the surface of the platform. There in front of him, was the Dark, that heaving mass of every wrong committed by humanity, now condensed into a thing powerful enough to rip vast holes between worlds and allow Hell through. It was still above the hole in the centre of the platform, and still the Dead were flowing into it, flapping and cracking into each other, sending great sprays of blood and innards into the air.

And at its very centre, hidden from view, was his father.

Lazarus knew what he had to do, that it might just kill him, and that he had no choice. And without even looking back to check on Arielle, he gritted his teeth and ran.

The Dead took no notice of him. They were too intent on being swept up into the Dark to realise that, coming at them as hard as he could, was the one person who could put an end to their lust for life, and bring everything crashing down around them.

Lazarus saw the hole in the platform coming up fast.

This was it, the do or die moment. His left foot landed just a few millimetres from the edge and, using the momentum he'd built up from the sprint, he launched himself into the stream of the Dead spewing out of the hole and into the Dark far above.

It was like he'd jumped into a geyser filled with corpses to drown in a slurry of dead, stinking flesh. The bodies had no control over themselves. Hands and arms and legs and faces smashed into him, and it was all Lazarus could do to fight them off and give himself enough room to breathe. As he rose higher, he could now see what the Dark had become. Before, it had been terrifying; a great and impossible thing, but with no real structure to it. Now it was so much more. The Dead, as they ascended, were absorbed by it and became a part of it. The Dark was a stinking, spinning, swirling swill of torn, shredded souls screaming out in agony, and it was a pain they seemed to be enjoying. Faces would come at Lazarus, stretching out of the Dark as though trying to push through the skin of a balloon. Hands would seek for him, but would be snatched back before they had a chance to reach him. And all the time he was still being sucked upwards. The Dark was spewing itself down the side of the tower, taking the Dead to the world below in a thick slurry of stinking, creeping death. He had to do something quickly before he ended up going the same way. But what?

Another face pushed out of the Dark and Lazarus let instinct take over, depending on the Keeper inside him, hoping somehow he'd know what he was doing.

With a ferocious heave, he brought the spike round in a swift, angry arc and rammed it right through the face as its mouth stretched, almost like it wanted to swallow him whole. He put everything into that stab, imagined it not just going through the creature, but right through the Dark, ripping it in two, bursting it so that he could get to his dad.

As the spike sunk in, Lazarus felt the same sensation he experienced when pulling the Dead out of a living body. Only this time, not only was it more intense, like every atom in his body was on fire, but it was driving through him and channelling itself down the weapon in his hand.

The mouth of the Dead froze in a half-scream, choking the rest of it down as thick black and red gore burst from the wounds either side of its head. It thrashed around in front of him, tried to dislodge the spike, but no way was it coming free. And as the thrashing grew more frantic, the skin of the Dark started to split. Soon it was peeling away in front of Lazarus, revealing behind it the Dead he'd skewered. Its head was gushing blood and gore now, spraying the stuff out like a burst artery. Lazarus had no choice but to just hang on and close his eyes as the stuff washed over him, pushed up his nose. The strain on his arms was agonising and as he yelled out, the rank slime spraying out from the head wounds he'd inflicted filled his mouth. Then the Dark shuddered. And everything, in an instant, fell still.

Below him, Lazarus heard the Dead scream. Still holding on to the spike rammed through the head of the creature, he looked down to see them tumbling back into each other, smashing and crashing bone and flesh into flesh and bone, breaking and snapping and bursting. And then the Dark slumped suddenly downwards, back to the platform, and Lazarus's stomach was left behind.

Closing his eyes and waiting for the inevitable impact on the platform, Lazarus was thankful that his fall was broken by a pile of the Dead. It was like being thrown on to a rubbish heap, except this was one that wanted to drag you inside. Hands grabbed him. Teeth bit into him. Arms wrestled him down. But Lazarus was having none of it and lashed out with his spike, rage spitting itself from his mouth, and he tumbled off the pile to the floor, not that he could see it. The platform was littered with a squirming, writhing blanket of the Dead, all those that had, moments earlier, been inside the Dark, ready to be unleashed on Earth. But now the Dark was no longer the hideous, spinning vortex. It was shrinking like a thick cloud being sucked into a vacuum cleaner. The sound of it was awful, like blubber being thrown into a shredder. And when that cloud had finally gone, all that remained of the Dark was a single person. A man standing across from Lazarus, waist deep in the Dead, his eyes hollow portals to Hell, his skin lined with thick, black lines like veins, which squirmed and twisted under his skin.

'Dad . . .'

The word slipped from Lazarus as, from behind him, he heard a shout and turned to see Arielle fighting countless Fallen. They were swooping in and out of each other, crashing on the platform only to leap back up again into the air for more of the same. How Arielle was keeping them at bay he couldn't imagine. She looked knackered, but still terrifying.

'Finish it, Lazarus!' Arielle yelled out. 'NOW!'

Lazarus snapped back round to his father, just in time to dodge a thick tentacle of the Dark that shot out from his body.

Another tentacle came crashing out, then another, but Lazarus managed to weave away from them, slashing at them with his spike. But he needed to get shifting; Arielle wouldn't be able to keep going for much longer and sooner or later one of those Dark tentacles was going to slap him into the afterlife. Lazarus looked across to his father. He hadn't come all this way to fail now. No way in Hell!

Another tentacle leapt forward, but this time Lazarus didn't duck. He crouched down, grabbed one of the Dead and waited until the tentacle was just about to wrap itself round him, then threw the screaming corpse as hard as he could.

The Dead screamed as the tentacle wrapped round it then squeezed it so tight that it burst like a tube of strawberry yogurt. Lazarus didn't wait around to watch. As the blood rained down he sprinted, his feet slipping and tripping and sinking into the squirming floor of corpses. His father was only a few steps away.

Lazarus dug deep, screamed and, with a final surge of energy, dragged from the very bottom of his soul, leapt forward in a death dive through the air.

32

A MESS TO BEHOLD

Letting go of the spike at the last moment, Lazarus clamped his hands on to his father's face. They sank into his flesh. It was the closest he'd been to him in years.

A shocked gasp caught in his father's throat and a scream ripped its way out. Lazarus momentarily closed his eyes to it, but that scream continued, and he was the cause of it. Eyes open, Lazarus wouldn't be letting go again, not until this was over for good.

Lazarus dragged every ounce of strength and energy he had and pushed it into his arms, forcing himself to fight against the struggle his dad was now putting up; his body was shaking so rapidly it was a blur, his limbs thrashing about, clawing at Lazarus, drawing blood. And the Dark was bursting out from him now in all directions, trying to grab on to Lazarus, but leaping away if it ever got close, almost as though to touch him was like being burned. Lazarus knew he had to stay in control. One false move, one hint that he didn't think he'd win this, and the Dark would have him and it would be over.

With a violent twist, he pulled his dad round and on to the ground, landing on top of him, pinning him to the moaning Dead underneath them. The Dead tried to get away from what was happening, but they couldn't escape and filled the air with their yells. Lazarus ignored them, focused on his dad, stared down at the face of the man he'd grown up with but hardly knew, the man whose life had been a lie, a hidden thing of horror and fear. And all of it tainted with a single tragedy, the death of his mum. This was finally it. This was where it ended!

With a roar that screamed out from his very soul, Lazarus reached inside his father for the slimy, wriggling, writhing thing that had him under its control. And he found it: the Dark!

Pain slammed into Lazarus, burning him from the inside out. But the Dark could not escape now. It burst from his father, a fountain of black liquid rods, flailing about like hair, whipping at Lazarus, pulling at him, stabbing him, cutting him till he was bleeding all over. But still he held on.

The Dark tried again, its movements more desperate and frantic, but Lazarus was in so much pain, he could feel no more. He was numb to it. Nothing could touch him now. And, with the Dark at his mercy, he ripped his hands away from his father's face, taking skin with them, but also the Dark, which spewed out black and fetid and foul.

Lazarus tumbled on to his back and the Dark, no longer inside his father, slumped on top of him like a giant bag filled with pus. He couldn't breathe, could hardly move, as the stuff began to work its way into every pore in his body, up his nose, into his ears, his mouth, even his eyes. The pain was indescribable, but in his desperate fight to get the stuff off, his left hand scraped across something a little familiar. He clasped it, gripped it hard, and in the last few moments before he was about to black out, twisted his body to the right, and brought the spike up and through the Dark, slicing it clean in two.

* * *

Lazarus opened his eyes. He was still on the floor, but the Dark was no longer on him, suffocating and drowning him. To his right stood Arielle. She was a mess to behold, her clothes in tatters, her body covered in cuts, blood everywhere. One eye was smashed in with such a bruise it was sealed shut with a weeping crust. And over her shoulder was the body of his father.

'Is he . . .'

Arielle, her face twitching in pain, simply turned and dropped from the platform go glide into dark sky.

Lazarus dragged himself to his knees only to hear a dark, rumbling growl. He sat back on his feet, looked to his side, and shuddered. There, in all his awful glory, was Red. Only now he wasn't so beautiful any more and it was all Lazarus could do to not turn away from him.

The angel, for angel he was as Lazarus had come to realise, was standing on a tumbling, twisting, writhing mass of teeth-covered tentacles. How many creatures there were, Lazarus couldn't say or even tell. He didn't want to know. He just wanted them to stay the hell away. That they were Red's pets and would not harm him was the only thing keeping him from collapsing in terror. Red himself was again a ruined thing of blood and flesh, the stuff torn from him in great strips. His wings were tattered and torn, like curtains in a burned-out building. But he was healing. Slowly. He opened his ruined mouth to reveal an ice-white grin of perfect teeth.

'You are, as always, a surprise, dear Lazarus,' he said, his voice almost melodic as he leaned forward a little to allow one of the tentacles which bore him to gently caress his cheek.

'Is that a compliment?'

'It is an observation, Keeper, nothing more.'

Lazarus stood. He ached like mad and could feel a wave of pain just waiting to come crashing down on him.

Red spoke again. 'Tobias is alive, Lazarus. Weak, but alive. His days as a Keeper are truly at an end. But perhaps, as a father they can now begin?'

Red's words came at Lazarus like a kick from a mule. Had he actually succeeded after all? He caught sight of his spike at his feet. He reached down, shook it free of the muck that had collected on it in the fight, and held it again in his hand, enjoying the sensation of the thorns sinking into his hand and out the other side. It felt good there, terribly so.

'What now?'

Red rested his chin in his hand. 'You will continue your father's work,' he said. 'You are the Keeper. And the Dead fear you Lazarus. As do I.'

Lazarus choked.

'There have been many before you, Lazarus,' said Red almost philosophically, 'but none like you. You could do great things. And terrible.'

Lazarus suddenly felt very aware of his age. He wasn't ready for this! There were things he wanted to do with his life. Having it already decided for him was not a part of the plan and never had been!

Then an image came to him and he was momentarily holding Clair as she stared up at him in her final moments.

What was it Arielle had said, something about all wars having their victims? Clair hadn't asked for the war, yet she had come along anyway and paid the ultimate sacrifice. Lazarus knew then that he had no choice; his path was set.

'The Dead will come again,' he said, looking up at Red. 'And worse. Things neither you nor I can even begin to imagine.'

'You see what I mean?' said Red sitting back, almost laughing. 'Keepers there have been, but none of them were like you! And you're right, Lazarus, I'm afraid. I fear that all of this is but a start of something. Your work as Keeper has only just begun and dark days lie ahead for you, of that I have no doubt.'

Lazarus nodded solemnly, accepting his fate at last.

'Enough of the talk,' said Red. 'The Fallen have been beaten back and are locked from the tower. Even now its light chases them. But the tower will soon slip from this world, back to where it belongs. And you must not be here when it does. Only I can go with it.'

Lazarus remembered the light, what it did, how it burned. But he couldn't feel sorry for the Fallen. They were damned for eternity by what they had done. And it was clear that given the slightest chance they'd do it again.

'The Dead?'

Red slipped closer still. 'That battle is close to ending

for the moment, at least. When the Dark fell, their hold on this world crumbled. Your friends have need of you, I'm sure, now that your work here is done.'

On those last fateful words, the tower shuddered.

'To me, Lazarus. Now!'

Red held out his hand and the creatures lowered him for Lazarus to take hold. When Lazarus didn't immediately reach out, Red snatched him from the platform and pulled him close. He was sticky and hot and smelled of rot and foulness. But for once it didn't make Lazarus gag or even feel dizzy. Then, with a guttural cry to the squirming creatures at his feet, Red splayed out his wings and sprang into the sky, Lazarus clamped as close to him as a child to its mother.

33
TWO WORDS

Like riding a cloud of eels, Lazarus and Red fell from the tower's platform on the creatures of oblivion. About them, the sky was slipping away to a normal darkness of distant stars. The exhilaration of the freefall sent Lazarus's stomach into a spin, and it felt good, was a sign that he was still alive!

With Red's arms around him, Lazarus stared back at the great black tower. Already it looked less stable, and faint motes of dust could be seen shooting out from between the black bricks as it shuddered. Below them, and with relief, he saw four figures: Abaddon, Arielle, Craig and James. Again, he remembered Clair, her absence dreadfully stark, but he couldn't dwell on it; if he did, he would be of little use to anyone. So he focused again and saw surrounding the four on the ground, on the road and in the fields, a carpet of bodies. For an awful moment, Lazarus thought they were corpses, that none of the festival goers had survived. But as they fell closer he could see that from the bodies the Dead were dragging themselves out in terrified desperation, and filling the air with yells of fear. His destruction of the Dark had, as Red had said, broken their hold, and now they wanted out. And fast. He remembered Matthew then, and his long wait for his daughter. Lazarus hoped they both lay out thee, the Dead leaving there at last.

He pointed to his friends. 'Your pets are hungry, right?'

Red roared, adjusted his course, and took them straight into the fight.

Lazarus leapt away from Red as they landed, and ran over to Craig. In his hands were the scythes Abaddon had given to him before they'd driven off the end of the pier and straight to Hell.

'I'd ask you how it went,' said Craig, turning to meet him, his whole body looking like he'd just walked through an abattoir. 'But looking at you I think

I could probably hazard a guess.'

To their left, a hand burst out of a still-breathing body and dragged with it a distorted, snarling head. It didn't get far as Craig cut it in two. Lazarus caught sight of Arielle and James doing the same, crushing the Dead as they emerged from the bodies they had inhabited. Abaddon, though, seemed distracted. Then he saw why; unlike all the others, and standing in the middle of the dreadful scene, was Mary.

'She's been like that the whole time,' said Craig, taking the head off another of the Dead. 'When you got rid of the Dark, everyone collapsed to the ground. We thought they were dead, but when the Dead started to try and escape, we found they were anything but. And we've been doing our best to keep on top of them. Some have got away though, I know that for a fact.'

'And Mary?'

'Like I said,' explained Craig, sounding suddenly exhausted, 'everyone dropped to the ground, but she didn't. And she hasn't moved since. Abaddon's been making his way slowly towards her. It won't be long now. Though what he'll do . . .'

Lazarus hushed Craig. Abaddon had reached his daughter.

What happened next took Lazarus back to when Arielle had, on Abaddon's signal, pulled the Defender off the road for him to reveal the Black Shard.

Abaddon removed his jacket then tore off his shirt. His awful dead skin glistened in the moonlight reflected off the lake. He then took that same small knife he'd used before and snipped at the stitches holding him together.

'Laz,' said Craig. 'What's he doing?'

Lazarus didn't answer as Abaddon, his chest now open, knelt down in front of his daughter. The girl still refused to move. Then, with a protective gentleness that only a father can have for his own child, he reached out for Mary and drew her close.

A blinding ring of fiery light flared outwards, sweeping across the remaining Dead, blasting them to nothing, and forcing Lazarus and the others to shield their eyes. When they looked again, Abaddon and his daughter were gone.

Lazarus didn't wait for permission and ran across to where Abaddon had been standing. Arielle was first to join him, soon followed by Red and Craig. James, clearly overcome with exhaustion, stayed where he was and sank to the ground, his head in his hands.

'He's gone,' said Arielle, and Lazarus couldn't help but notice the faint note of sorrow in her voice. 'And if there are two people more deserving of the peace only death can bring, I don't yet know them.'

On the ground, where Abaddon and his daughter had stood, were two faint scorch marks. Already the wind was erasing them, but for a moment, Lazarus was sure that what he'd seen in them was the faint image of a man holding a child.

'What about the Black Shard?' said Craig.

'Gone for good, I think,' said Red.

'But why did she wait for him?' asked Lazarus. 'Why did she remain standing when everyone else collapsed?'

'Perhaps,' said Arielle, 'Mary was still in there somewhere. And perhaps she managed to hold on long enough for her father to at last take her home.'

It was then that Lazarus noticed his own father was missing from Arielle's shoulder. He swept his eyes round, suddenly desperately worried, as though someone could still come in and steal his father away from him at this last moment.

'Your father's in safe hands,' said Red. 'Over there, on the road. Look.'

Lazarus saw then what Red was talking about; a battered trailer attached to an old farm tractor. He recognised both. And the two figures in the back next to the enormous dog.

'When the Dark fell, I sent for him,' said Arielle. 'Figured we'd be needing some transport seeing as you seem to have misplaced my Defender.'

'Oh, that,' said Lazarus. 'Well, it's not misplaced. It's just not here either.'

Lazarus remembered wondering just how lucky they'd been that Willie had turned up after the crash, thinking that Arielle, perhaps, had had something to do with it. Seeing the kindly farmer here now only increased his wonder at what Arielle could do, her power.

'But isn't it a risk?' he asked. 'You know, having Willie knowing and seeing all this?'

Arielle's face was solemn. 'Whether we like it or not, this is not the kind of thing to go unnoticed.'

Lazarus was taken back to his conversation with Red before they had leapt from the tower. His future was seeming darker by the minute.

The sound of stone falling rumbled in the air. Everyone turned to look at the tower. It still stood, tall and wrong, stabbing out of the lake and into the sky. The rumbling came again, and Lazarus saw black stone starting to fall.

'It's losing its hold on this world,' said Arielle. 'It will soon fall.'

There was sorrow in her voice and he saw her glance across to Red, who, despite his ruined face, managed a smile of such warmth and love that Lazarus understood then why Arielle hid so much in the drink she always had close by. She then moved over to Red's side and held his hand.

More stones fell. The tower had little time left, and Lazarus could now see it sinking back beneath the water.

A blur of movement caught his eye, and when he looked he saw Arielle standing alone, and the shrinking silhouette of Red on the wing speeding towards the tower. When he reached it, the place shuddered violently, almost as though his weight had jolted it. Then last, and with the sound of continental plates colliding, the tower sank beneath the waves, and was gone.

Arielle stared out across the lake, her arms wrapped around herself, her wings now faded from sight once more.

Lazarus heard a voice call for him. He turned from the lake and saw his father lift up a hand and give him a tentative wave.

He walked over, leaving Craig with Arielle to go and see to James. At the trailer, his dad attempted a smile. Pain tried to break it, but somehow it held on, flickering a little, like it wasn't used to being seen, didn't know how to react.

This was the moment that Lazarus had held on to all along and, Keeper or not, he smiled back with two words he'd never before said with any warmth or love.

Until now.

'Hi . . . Dad.'

ACKNOWLEDGEMENTS

It's been a hell of a ride writing The Dead/Dark/Damned. So here's to those who've stuck with me on the trail, no matter how dark and bloody . . .

My Glorious Gory Gatwards: It's not easy living with a writer. Well done on not killing me. Yet . . .

The Hodder Hell Hounds: Words fail . . . so I hope a severed head will do. It's in the post . . .

Dan 'I walk like a pigeon' Kelly: Best impromptu Bed and Breakfast in the London-London I know of.

Lex 'best name in show business' Shrapnel: It's good to know someone who gets the idiotic life I'm now leading. And if anything of mine gets screen time, you get first dibs on the major roles . . .

The Trapped By Monsters Posse and the Chainsaw Gang: You help my life stay weird. I like that.

The writers I read: Clive 'Hellbound Heart' Barker, Stephen 'Salem's Lot' King, Peter 'Ghost Story' Straub, Jack 'The Lost' Ketchum, Gary 'Mr Hands' Braunbeck, Boston 'God is a Bullet' Teran, Joe '20th Century Ghosts' Hill, Simon 'Blood Crazy' Clark, HP 'The Call of Cthulhu' Lovecraft, Neal 'The Skinner' Asher, Graham 'Smoking Poppy' Joyce.

The music I write to: Black Sabbath, Mudvayne, SOAD, Nirvana, MCR, Disturbed, Burt Jansch, Earth, Battery Cage, The Rosedales, John Martyn, Mastodon, Of skin and Saliva, Deutsch Nepal, Nick Cave, In Slaughter Natives, Miles Davis, Tindersticks, Devil Driver, Focus.

And finally . . .

My Blood-soaked Deadlings: You people are the force behind this, believing in it, loving it, keeping the Facebook and Twitter thing rockin' and rollin', screaming for more . . . Thanks to you all, but a special mention to the Unfortunate Few lucky enough to win a place on this page . . . Mark 'Spider' Little, Darren 'Death by Reviews' Hartwell, Holly 'Creepy Auzzie Lady' Harkness, Cameron 'US Deadlings Fansite' Dukes, Richard 'First

US Dead Fan' Gingrich, Shay 'The Dead are coming' Dickson, Tony 'Insane Bookseller' Higginson, Katie 'Dodgy Horror Movies' Richardson, Emma 'I do shorthand' Stokes, Connor 'Hell, Lazarus' Spangfort, Keith 'They seeped' Walters, Kieran 'Crystal ball and black cape' Ferris-Bureau, Nellie 'Would I dye it this colour?' Walters, Usaamah 'I got The Dark from the library' Khan.

ABOUT THE AUTHOR

David was born in Bristol and grew up with his two younger brothers between the Cotswolds, Wensleydale and Lincolnshire. Aside from having a huge number of hobbies including: caving, camping, climbing, archery, shooting and music, David also wrote avidly. Although he had his first book published aged 18, it's taken many more years and life experiences to lead to writing *The Dead*. Seeing two ghosts, being mistaken for a homeless person and almost drowning have given David plenty of food for thought, but it's his family who've been a big inspiration. Now living in rural Somerset with his wife and two boys, David writes full-time and hopes to see ghost number three very shortly.

Questions and Answers with David Gatward

What do you enjoy most about writing a book?

You're playing God! Seriously – you're immersed in a world that you created, running around with characters you dreamt up, battling evil ... and winning! When you realise the story is working, that the characters are as real as they could get, you find the story just starts racing ahead and you have to keep up. It's strangely exciting, a bit weird and scary, and completely enthralling. I cannot express how lucky I am to be in a position to be writing books. It's astonishing.

What do you least like about writing a book?

The fear of knowing you've got to come up with a story can be terrifying – the fear of the blank page/screen. Those days when nothing happens in your head, when it takes hours and hours and hours to come up with just a few hundred words, and each one of them really, really hurt. Deadlines approaching too fast. The fear of failure haunting you with each book you write, that it'll be total junk and the world will laugh at you and force you to wear pants on your head for the rest of your life.

Writing seems to be a very solitary occupation – are you someone who's comfortable with his own company?

Yes. But that doesn't mean I'm a hermit in a cave with a crab as my only mate. Writers need solitude to get on with it. But I've trained myself to find that anywhere (I wrote a book on train journeys over a period of five weeks). I write with the world blocked out, but when I'm not writing I love being around the people that make my life fizz and buzz and thump.

What was your favourite book as a child?

The one which sticks with me is *The Weirdstone of Brisingamen*, by Alan Garner. It has this one bit in it, where the heroes end up crawling through a water-filled tunnel and they have no choice but to go through it, not knowing if they'll get out or drown. It still haunts me today!

Have you ever seen a ghost?

Yes, I have seen a ghost. Well two, actually. The first, a man dressed all in black, appeared one sunny morning while I was mowing a lawn. Didn't say much; just stared. Kind of freaked me out though. The second, a woman in a blue dress, woke me up in the middle of the night while I was living in a caravan (which, just so you know, was situated on what was once an old graveyard). Pretty weird, particularly as, despite it being dark out, inside, the caravan was all lit up.

Who are your heroes?

I don't have any in the conventional sense, but I do have a few people I admire. These include (in no specific order): my dad, an old friend Michael Forster, and writers Linda Chapman and Neil Gaiman.

What do you do in your spare time?

As I'm making the transition from full-time yawn-filled job, to full-time 'WOW!' writing, I don't really have spare time! But in the bits I find, I hang out with family/friends, read, listen to music, cook ... and try to work out if I'll ever have time again to do stuff like play the drums, go climbing, go to the gym ...

What's your guilty pleasure?

Glee!

What's your dream car?

Landrover Defender 110 King Cab (done out to my own spec, obviously).

If you were a superhero, what would your power be?

The ability to fly. That sense of freedom, to be able to just take off and zip through the sky ... I'd so totally love that.

What is your perfect sandwich?

Er ... well, this is the one I have late at night: peanut butter, mayonnaise, Danish blue cheese, sliced onion, and cheese and onion crisps. Yeah, I know ...

ANTHONY

HOROWITZ HORROR

Collection of horror stories by No 1 bestselling author Anthony Horowitz.

It's a world where everything seems pretty normal. But the weird, the sinister and the truly terrifying are lurking just out of sight. Like an ordinary-looking camera with evil powers, a bus ride home that turns into your worst nightmare and a mysterious computer game that nobody would play... if they knew the rules!

ORCHARD BOOKS
www.orchardbooks.co.uk

KITE IDENTITY

BOOK ONE SOFT TARGETS

LUKE KITE HAS SPENT HIS LIFE ESTRANGED FROM HIS MULTI-BILLIONAIRE FATHER AND HIS HALF SISTER MEGAN.

AFTER HIS FATHER'S DEATH HOWEVER, LUKE AND MEGAN ARE DRAWN TOGETHER IN A TERRIFYING GAME OF CAT AND MOUSE.

FROM LONDON, THROUGH NEW YORK TO TOKYO, A DANGEROUS WEB OF LIES AND DECEIT UNRAVELS, AND THE KITE IDENTITY IS REVEALED...

KITE IDENTITY
BOOK ONE SOFT TARGETS
A BOND THAT CAN NEVER BE BROKEN
HARRY EDGE

Hodder Children's Books

www.hodderchildrens.co.uk

THE RECRUIT

Robert Muchamore

Book 1 – OUT NOW

The Recruit tells James's story from the day his mother dies. Read about his transformation from a couch potato into a skilled cherub agent.

Meet Lauren, Kerry and the rest of the CHERUBS for the first time, and learn how James foiled the biggest terrorist massacre in British history.

The first explosive CHERUB mission.

www.cherubcampus.com